THE ROAD TO AGRA

Special Notice to Book Club Members

This book is a selection of the WEEKLY READER CHILDREN'S BOOK CLUB. It was chosen especially for our members by the Weekly Reader Selection Board after careful consideration of hundreds of other books for girls and boys.

Members of the WEEKLY READER CHILDREN'S BOOK CLUB receive six or more exciting books during the year—including one or more Free Bonus Books upon joining. They also receive a Membership Certificate, Club Bookmarks and regular Book Club Bulletins.

We hope you enjoy this book. Your friends will enjoy it, too. If they are not already members, why not ask them to join the WEEKLY READER CHILDREN'S BOOK CLUB.

WEEKLY READER
Children's Book Club
Education Center • Columbus 16, Ohio

THE

ROAD

TO

AGRA

By AIMÉE SOMMERFELT

ILLUSTRATED BY *Ulf Aas*

CRITERION BOOKS

NEW YORK

WEEKLY READER
Children's Book Club
Edition, 1962

First American edition 1961

English translation copyright © 1961 by Criterion
Books, Inc., and University of London Press, Ltd.

Library of Congress Catalog Card Number: 61-12805

This book was originally published in 1959 by N. W. Damm & Son,
Oslo, Norway, under the title Veien til Agra.

Manufactured in the United States of America
By American Book–Stratford Press, Inc.

Designed by Sidney Feinberg

CONTENTS

1   LALU IS FORCED TO MAKE A DECISION   11

2   THE NIGHT ON THE ROOF   21

3   THE GURU AND THE MONEYLENDER   33

4   WHAT HAPPENED IN ALLAHABAD   45

5   JHANDU, THE CAMEL DRIVER   59

6   IN A BAOLI   75

7   THE ELEPHANT   84

8   THE SIGNALMAN   95

9   THE LITTLE WEAVERS   113

10   THE BOY WITH THE BICYCLE   126

11   THE SOCIETY FOR COMBATING BLINDNESS   141

12   THE ECHO   155

13   THE GRAY ELEPHANT   169

14   MONKEYS IN THE APPLE ORCHARD   180

   Glossary   189

WEEKLY READER

CHILDREN'S BOOK CLUB

THE ROAD TO AGRA

1

LALU IS FORCED TO MAKE A DECISION

Lalu lived in a village called Katwa, which was just like all the other villages in India, and this morning began exactly like all other mornings.

Lalu went to the well to fetch water. He hadn't a thought in his head, least of all of going to Agra. In front of him ran Kanga, a thin, gray dog who could dance to music and walk on tiptoe.

As a puppy, Kanga had been trained in a circus. Later she was stolen by a man who intended to earn money by showing her off, but Kanga refused to dance to the man's pipe. She bit his leg and then ran away. Driven by hunger, she came one day to the house where Lalu lived and remained there. Lalu christened her Kanga and secretly divided his food with her. After that he could not go anywhere without Kanga following him. True, Kanga would not dance or walk on tiptoe, at any rate not when anyone asked her to do so. She only danced when it was least expected, for she was a self-willed dog. She suited Lalu well, for he was a self-willed boy.

Lalu half ran, half walked, with the water pitcher on his head and Kanga leading the way. His feet raised little clouds of red dust as he ran. Just before he crossed the highway he met his friend Kamak. They stopped, put down their water pitchers and began talking together. Kamak was chewing a piece of sugar cane and was in the mood for a chat.

"In Agra," he said, "there is a hospital where they make sick eyes well again."

"Nonsense," said Lalu.

"In Agra," insisted Kamak, "there is a doctor who heals sick eyes. He is more clever than any other doctor in the whole of India."

"How do you know that?" said Lalu skeptically.

"My uncle came home yesterday. He can see as well as you and I."

Lalu was amazed. Kamak's uncle had been practically blind and had sat for over a year on the station steps, holding out his beggar's cup along with all the other beggars.

"Can he see? Has he no need to beg any longer?"

"I tell you, he sees as well as you or I."

Thoughts began to tumble about in Lalu's head. He began to see a light in the darkness that had been surrounding him.

"Maya," he said involuntarily.

His sister Maya's eyes grew worse every year and even with every change of the moon. The family tried to keep the fact a secret from the neighbors because Maya had been promised a place in a school in a nearby village where they could take in only a few beginners. If the teacher heard of Maya's bad eyes he would give her place to some other seven year old. There were plenty of them wanting it.

No one in the family spoke about her eyes, even among

themselves. It was as if they thought they could make them healthy again by keeping still about them.

Lalu had a special reason to fear that Maya might be turned away. He had decided that every word and every letter that Maya learned he would learn also. Nothing would get into Maya's head that did not get into his, too. This he had sworn to himself. A boy had to be sure of himself in this world since there were far too many young ones about.

"Get your father to take Maya to Agra," said Kamak, chewing his sugar cane. "There is a doctor there who . . ."

"Don't talk nonsense," said Lalu. "He wouldn't dare leave me and my little brothers to plant all the rice. What good would it do if Maya's eyes were healed, but we had no rice this autumn?"

"Well, let your mother go." Kamak said this lightly, for other people's troubles are not heavy to bear and even poor people are rich in advice.

"Mother? With a new baby and two other little ones?"

Kamak bit into the sugar cane with his white teeth and laughed: "Why don't you take her yourself?"

"On foot all the way to Agra?" Lalu laughed, too, as if it were a joke, took his pitcher and went on. He had had enough of good advice.

It was early morning. A wreath of light white clouds lay along the horizon, but higher up the sky was clear and blue. Not until later in the day did the sky become white and colorless from the heat, causing both men and beasts to seek the shade. From the highway, which stretched straight out in front of Lalu, came the hooting of cars pushing through the crowded traffic of ox-drawn carts, camels and bicycles.

This was the highroad to Agra.

If only he had a bicycle! Or if his father could spare him an ox from the plowing! Then he could easily get to Agra with Maya. At one time his father had had a horse and two cows tied up in his yard, but that was a long time ago, before the year of great famine.

Lalu broke into a run to get across the open treeless bit of land before the heat became too strong, but when he had crossed the highroad he stopped and looked toward the west.

The road stretched before him, endlessly long, losing itself in mist on the horizon. Each passing car raised thick clouds of dust which slowly settled on the pedestrians and the drivers. Rows of mango trees bordered the road, and large apes sat in the branches, gazing at the traffic. The apes were gray, the trees were gray, and gray was the road leading across the flat, burned-up plain.

One could walk along such a road until one dropped or was pounced upon by wild beasts some pitch black night. Or one could step by accident on a snake. It would be madness to try to do what Kamak had proposed so lightly, as if walking to Agra with a seven-year-old sister was something he himself did every day of the year.

Lalu stood still, thinking deeply: "We could take Surmi with us, and then Maya could ride," he thought.

The donkey Surmi was thirteen years old, just like himself, but thirteen years was a great age for a thin donkey. Surmi was not of very much use. Would he have the strength to get to Agra and back? Oh, yes! donkeys are very tough.

Perhaps he, Lalu, *could* save those eyes on which so much depended for them both. For even if Maya were able to get into school by pretending that she could see as well as the others, would she be able to fool the teacher? Would she be able to learn anything with her bad eyes?

"We could sleep under a tree with the donkey as a pillow . . . and of course we must have Kanga with us."

Lalu wondered just how dangerous the road to Agra was at night, when darkness fell and all children had to stay indoors. Often, when he couldn't sleep at night, he heard the jackals out on the plain. What a hungry sound their howling was! It was as if they shrieked with their bellies, said Nani. They were cowardly in the day, but bold at night. One or two might not be dangerous, but when there were hundreds of them, and all starving—what then?

He walked on slowly and turned into the path leading to the well. The sun burned him as soon as he was out of the shade, but he went straight on keeping his head immovable beneath the water pitcher. Inside his head the thoughts buzzed like bees in a beehive which has been hit by a stone.

"Mother cannot leave the little ones and Father cannot leave the rice. Nani is too old. I must do it. And I am afraid. I cannot. I cannot. I am only brave in the daytime."

There were a number of people around the well even though it was early. Some of the women knelt close to the pond, beating their washing with flat, bat-like sticks. Two oxen, with bandages over their eyes, walked around and around, turning the great, creaking wooden wheel which was fitted with buckets which came up full of water from the depths of the well. Such oxen have done this work for centuries on end in India. The water streamed out fresh and cold from the buckets on the wheel, out into the pond where the women were washing and the animals drinking. Everyone was talking and shouting.

Lalu saw his mother who was busy spreading out the finished washing on the grass so that the sun might dry it before she took it home. The baby lay in the shade a few yards away. The donkey, Surmi, who was to carry the washing home on his back, was also there, standing with his hoofs in the water and drinking. Beside Surmi, holding his reins, stood Maya.

At first she did not see Lalu. She was standing very

still with her head bent, for she felt insecure among so many people. She was wearing a pair of long, wide cotton trousers with a three-quarter-length red blouse reaching down to her knees. She was too small to wear a sari like her mother. She had long, dark braids and blue eyes which were the pride of the family, for blue eyes are rare in India. Maya was very pretty, and the only daughter among four brothers.

Lalu whistled a little signal. Maya lifted her head and looked around but could not see her brother until he was quite close to her. Then she made a quick movement, threw the reins over the back of Surmi and ran toward him. Half blind as she was, she stumbled over a basket full of clean clothes which one of the women had just gathered together after the half-hour drying time in the sun. The basket upset and the clothes fell into the muddy water which the animals had been drinking.

What a fuss and to-do! The woman to whom the clothes belonged waved her arms and scolded, someone else laughed, someone else made loud remarks, and in the middle of all the turmoil, Kanga took it into her head to do a little dance and walk on tiptoe. All the noise no doubt made her think she was in the circus.

Maya crept close to Lalu. She was terrified and bewildered, for she knew she had been the cause of all the trouble. Their mother ran toward them and the angry woman immediately showered her with abuse.

"Just look what happens when someone brings a half-blind kid to the well."

"Maya is not half-blind," said her mother in defense. "She sees very well and helps me a lot in the house."

"Sees very well, does she? Why did she do this then?"

"I'll rinse out the clothes for you," shouted the mother. "An accident can happen to anyone. Quiet, Kanga, quiet!"

For Kanga had stopped dancing and had begun to bark, adding to the general hullabaloo around the well.

"Take the child and that mad cur away with you," shouted an angry man. "They're both of them equally stupid."

"Sees quite well, does she?" mocked a mother who had a boy Maya's age. "And a kid like that is going to get a place in the school. Keeping out others with perfectly good eyes!"

"What do children want to go to school for," growled the angry man. "They only get swollen heads, and won't stay at home and help their parents. The wise man never reads a book."

"He's right, he's certainly right," said many.

"I'll rinse out your clothes for you," repeated the mother helplessly. She could think of nothing else to say.

Nothing worse could possibly have happened. Now the whole village would know that Maya's eyes had grown weaker.

"I'll report it to the schoolmaster. That sort of thing must not happen," shouted another mother who also had a child who wanted to go to school.

"Don't do that," said Lalu. "Maya is going to Agra to have her eyes cured."

"To Agra! Ha, ha! And who is going to take her there, if I may be allowed to ask?"

"I am," said Lalu.

2

THE NIGHT ON THE ROOF

When Lalu came running home with the water pitcher, the smoke from the village lay heavily over the low, chimneyless houses, hiding them in shadow. He was panting and snorting like a tired little buffalo. Behind him came Kanga, her tongue hanging out. There was not really any reason to hurry, but Lalu had run all the way home in the burning sun. His mind had made him run, and it was his mind that had made him decide to take Maya to Agra. He had announced his decision before he himself really knew what he was saying. Oh, he would show them! They were all so stupid. That's what they were—stupid. They wouldn't have their way and keep Maya out of school. Not if he could help it!

He ran into the sun-baked yard with its outdoor fireplace, where he found Nani cooking pancakes on a stone hearth while she fanned the smoke away with a peacock feather fan. Lalu put the water pitcher in the shadow of the wall, and only then did he realize that it was empty.

He had been so angry, he had forgotten to fill it. He wiped the sweat from his forehead and went over to the fireplace.

Nani looked up and noticed the deep frown between his eyes as she handed him a newly-baked pancake.

"Have you been up to something, boy? An empty pitcher and a frown on your forehead."

"Nani," said Lalu, "I'm going to walk to Agra and take Maya with me."

Nani threw another pancake onto the warm stones and did not seem as surprised as Lalu had expected. That annoyed him. One did not make such an important

decision as this every day, and at least people could stop baking pancakes when they heard the news.

He broke off a bit of the cake and gave it to Kanga while he swallowed the rest.

"I'm going to take Surmi with me," he said, "and Kanga of course, because she will help to keep the jackals away at night."

Nani fanned her old face with the peacock fan.

"Let us talk about all this, Lalu," she said. "Tell me what has happened."

Those were words that Lalu liked. Grownups never seemed to want to talk things over; they only liked to give orders.

He told his grandmother all that had happened that morning, about Kamak's uncle who had had his sight restored, about the accident at the well and the disdainful way in which the neighbors had treated his family. Yes, they even wanted to stop Maya from beginning school. But then he had told them all quite suddenly that he was going to take her to Agra.

"So you want Maya to be cured like Kamak's uncle? That is very good of you, Lalu, whether it can be managed or not," said Nani.

"I did not say it because I felt good," said Lalu. "I said it because I was so angry."

"One will be judged according to what one *does*," said Nani.

"Besides, I want to learn all that Maya learns in school."

Lalu had always hung about the other boys and girls who had been admitted to the school in the neighboring village, asking them to tell him all about the fine things they were learning—letters, numbers, and so on. But they were always so superior, and kept to themselves, making him feel left out. With Maya it would be different. Maya would be glad to share what she learned with him.

"Do you think I'll be allowed to take her, Nani?"

Nani threw another pancake onto the hearthstone and waved away the smoke with her peacock fan.

"It will be very difficult, Lalu."

"But I said it aloud at the well, Nani. I shouted it so that everyone heard it. Now I must go to Agra."

Nani did not say that it was dangerous or stupid or impossible for a child to do a thing like that. She said none of the things that he knew that his father or mother would say. On the contrary, she said:

"As pilgrims walk halfway across India to get to the Holy River Ganges, I see no reason why you should not go to Agra to get Maya's eyes cured."

"But do you think I am big enough to manage it, Nani?"

"It does not depend on size. The thin branch that bends is stronger than the thick one that cracks."

Lalu became almost terrified when he heard his grandmother talk like this—it was so unexpected. She did not produce a single argument against the trip, or even the very smallest objection. He had thought out answers to so many objections as he ran home from the well, and then there were no objections to answer.

He could do nothing but produce them himself.

"But Maya is only seven years old, Nani."

"The pilgrims are often younger. You must go carefully, that is all. Each of us must fly according to the size of his wings."

"She is very short-sighted and might step on a snake."

"That would be better than to go through her life as a blind beggar. Besides, the snakes generally come out only in the wet season, as you know."

Mother arrived home now with Maya and the two small brothers, driving Surmi in front of her loaded down with all the washing. She carried the baby on her hip and was very tired after all the trouble with the angry villagers and her efforts to calm them down.

"You should not have answered the people as you did down at the well, Lalu. You only make yourself ridiculous if you say things like that."

Lalu clenched his teeth and did not answer. He would prove to them that he did *not* make himself ridiculous. He would show her and all the others too.

"And then you forgot to bring the water. Go back at once and fill your pitcher!"

"May I wait until after we have eaten, Mother?"

"You propose to walk the whole way to Agra, but hesitate about going back to the well?"

Lalu took up his pitcher and went, but he couldn't

remember ever being so angry so often on one day before. He decided to speak to his father as soon as possible, while he still had the courage.

But when his father returned later in the day with the plowing oxen, tired and hungry, he would not listen to such nonsense. Lalu and Maya go to Agra? Never.

"God will never allow Maya to go blind unless it is ordained that she *shall* go blind," he scolded.

"Then He will help the children to make the journey if it is so ordained," Nani declared. She was the only one who dared speak to him when he was both hungry and tired. "And you have an uncle living in Agra. He would be a good help in getting Maya into the hospital."

"It is a long way to that uncle and I have not seen him for many years. And Lalu is a hasty and thoughtless boy. He has no patience."

"He who has patience may easily lose it on a long journey. But he who has none, like Lalu, can perhaps acquire it. A journey such as this may make a man of Lalu."

So said Nani. She dished out a bowl of rice for Father, made him sit down comfortably beside the fireplace and told Lalu and his little brothers to carry the day's food out to the buffaloes in the stable.

The hay was stacked in one corner of the yard and the boys carried small and large armfuls to the animals while Father was eating.

Agra was not mentioned again the whole of that day

until the sun went down, when Father came home for good and calm fell upon the household. At dusk a neighbor came in to have a chat by the fire. Father told him that Lalu had come up with the mad idea of going to Agra on foot so as to get Maya's eyes cured. He did this in the hope that the neighbor would shake his head and say, "Whatever will boys be up to next!" But the neighbor did not shake his head, for the neighbor had seen Kamak's uncle. And it was a miracle to see a man who had been as good as blind restored to sight. He told them that he had heard about the hospital in Agra and said that next week he was going to drive his oxen to the market at Allahabad and that Lalu and Maya were welcome to come with him on that part of the journey if they wished.

Father looked on this as a good omen. He began to consider the idea more seriously and at last he decided to ask the advice of the Guru, the holy man of the district, as all pious Indians do when a big decision has to be made. After that he went to bed.

The whole family slept out of doors. Lalu took his sleeping mat down from the wall and went up on the roof with Kanga. He slept on the roof every night. A tall tree stood close to the wall of the house, casting its shadow over the house most of the day, and where the shadow had fallen, the roof was not so hot to the touch. On this cool spot Lalu put his sleeping mat, pulled off his shirt, and enjoyed the coolness of the night with every pore of his body. No maharajah, no great man, no one in the whole world had such a good sleeping place as he had.

Small green parrots chattered in the tree top above him. Lalu lay on his back on his sleeping mat with Kanga beside him and hunted for the star pictures he knew so well. The man fighting the oxen. The Dog. He looked for the face of the moon god in the moon, and found it. The blanket of stars hung so low that he almost felt he could touch them. Everything was written in the stars— when he was born, when he would die, whether anything would come of this journey which he so longed to make, but which he dreaded at the same time and would even be glad to escape. If only he could interpret the stars! But the only person who could do that was the Guru to whom Father was going tomorrow morning. He would tell them whether the journey was advisable or not.

Suddenly the bamboo steps leading up to the roof creaked and a head appeared. It was Maya. She looked about for him in the darkness with those weak eyes of hers.

"Lalu! Are you there, Lalu? I can't sleep. Can I come up here to you?"

Lalu pushed the sleeping Kanga aside and made room for Maya on the mat. She came pattering across the roof on her bare feet.

"Why can't you sleep, Maya?"

"My eyes are hurting me. They are smarting."

Lalu rubbed her back. The smart was not there, of course, but he could not rub her eyes.

"They will soon be better, Maya. Shut your eyes and go to sleep."

"All right," said Maya. She laid her head on her arm and shut her eyes.

"Do you think we'll be eaten by jackals if we go on this journey, Lalu?"

"Of course not!" said Lalu, as he went on rubbing her back. "The jackals sneak into the villages and steal little children. You are not a little child, nor am I. Jackals are only dangerous to sick and helpless people."

"Tell me a story, Lalu. I have so many unhappy thoughts in my head tonight."

Lalu stopped rubbing her back, and began to tell her the story of the boy in the well:

"Once upon a time there was a famine in India, not the great famine when everybody died, but a small one when only children and old people died. In a village close to the jungle lived a boy called Nanak. He was big and strong and could thresh corn longer than anyone else without getting tired. But that year there was no corn to thresh, for the drought had burned up both the summer corn and the wet season corn, and still the rain would not come."

"Have you heard this story before, Maya?"

"Yes, Lalu. But I should like to hear it again."

So Lalu went on:

"Nanak went into the jungle to try to find roots and honey to eat. He walked and walked through the under-growth and the high grass, while the monkeys shrieked

at him from the trees and threw branches and twigs
down on his head. But he found no honey or roots he
could eat.

"At last he came to a deserted castle, all overgrown,
with many deep wells in which there was now no water.
A rich maharajah lived there once, but the water had
become tainted, and all his people had had to flee. Nanak
walked around looking at the fine buildings where only
snakes now lived. He shouted and heard his voice echo
back from the walls. Suddenly he was answered by a
wild elephant who broke out of the jungle and came
tramping toward him across the open space. Nanak
knew that it was dangerous to meet wild elephants on
open ground, so he hid himself in the main well of the
castle, which lay in the middle of the clearing. A banyan
tree had sent its roots down into the well, and Nanak
took hold of them and climbed down into it. Below him
slithered many snakes, and above him bellowed the
elephant. And a black and white mouse was gnawing the
root on which he hung so that at any moment he might
fall down to the snakes.

"But up in the banyan tree there hung a lovely comb
of honey, and when the elephant shook the tree the
honey ran down and Nanak licked it. Never had he tasted
such wonderful honey. It must be lotus honey, he
thought, honey that the bees had obtained from holy
flowers! It made him strong and patient so that he was
able to hold out until the elephant grew tired of bellow-

ing at him and went back into the jungle. Then he climbed up the wall of the well and chased away the black and white mouse who was gnawing the branches on which he had hung. Without paying any attention to the bees he pushed the whole comb of honey down into his sack, hoisted it onto his back, and went home. When he got home it was raining. And there was honey enough for everyone.

"Nanak never forgot the honey which had dripped into his mouth when everything was at its worst for him. For if things are at their worst there is always something good, somewhere, even if it is nothing but a drop of honey."

"Are you asleep, Maya?"

"No, Lalu. That was a fine story."

For a long time all was silent. Lalu heard only the grasshoppers in the hedge of cactus and the frogs in the canal croaking in the moonlight. He thought Maya was asleep, but in a little while she said to him:

"Mother thinks if we go to Agra we shall starve and go thirsty and be stung by cactus plants or chased by angry people. Do you think so too, Lalu?"

"Of course we shall," said Lalu yawning. "But it won't be so bad as losing the sight of both your eyes."

"No, Lalu." She lay still and thought. Then she added: "I'm afraid of cactuses and angry people."

"Yes, I understand that. But there are no cactuses and angry people here at this moment. Can't you wait to be frightened until we meet them? I want to go to sleep now."

"Yes, Lalu. But what if Father says no, and we are not allowed to go to Agra. I don't want to go blind."

"First of all you are afraid of going to Agra," cried Lalu, "and then you are afraid of not going. You know that the Guru asks the stars, and if they say we can go it will be all right. Go to sleep now, Maya."

"Yes, Lalu," said Maya. Then she went to sleep.

Lalu threw himself over onto his back and lay with his face toward the stars. If only he could interpret them. The frogs who had been croaking all evening were silent now, but he heard the hungry howls of the jackals out on the plain. They made Kanga lift her head and growl. To Lalu these sounds were like a greeting from the future whose meaning he could not understand.

3

THE GURU AND THE MONEY-LENDER

The Hindus in India worship a god just as we do in the West, but not a single God like ours. Their god has a hundred names, and a hundred forms, and each family chooses the one they like best. In Lalu's and Maya's home they had a shrine dedicated to Chaya, the goddess of shade and of mercy, and they thought that it was she who made the sun go down in the evening so that the earth would not be burned up.

Every morning when the family had washed themselves—and the washing was a part of their worship—they all gathered around the holy shrine while Nani rang a little temple bell.

"Blessed be thou," said Nani, her head bowed, and then they all prayed to Chaya, asking her to help them during the day.

This morning their father put on a newly-washed dhoti, combed his hair and took Lalu and Maya with him to visit the Guru. They left Kanga behind, tied to the fence, for they could not take dogs with them when they went to see such holy people as gurus.

When they went, Kanga tugged at her rope and whined.

The Guru was a very old man, dressed entirely in yellow. He had read the stars when both Lalu and Maya were born, and as soon as he heard what they had come for, he went off into a side room to study what he had written down at their birth. When he came back he went over to the flower-bedecked holy shrine in the corner of the room and fetched a small box with a tiny looking glass set into the lid. The box had belonged to another holy man and it was possible to see the future in it, the Guru said.

He handed the box to Lalu.

"What do you see in the glass, Lalu?"

Lalu stared into the looking glass where all sorts of colors and lights changed and intermingled.

"I see a yellow mustard field, I think, and a crawling snake."

"Shake the box," said the Guru. "What do you see now?"

Lalu shook the box and looked in the glass.

"I see a road."

"That's good. And what more?"

"Something big and gray. It might be a big gray elephant."

"Will she get her sight back?" asked their father impatiently. "Tell me if she will get her sight back."

"Shake the box again," said the Guru. "What do you see now?"

"Now I see nothing at all," said Lalu.

The Guru took the box and put it back in its place.

"Watch for a gray elephant," he said to Lalu. "It may bring you luck." Turning to the children's father, he went on:

"Whether Maya will get her sight back again or not I cannot say, but the journey lies in a fortunate phase of the moon, so I think it may be successful. Lalu could not see the journey home and I myself know little about it. Therefore it is not advisable for the children to come back on foot. I can say no more than that."

But that was enough for Lalu's father. He thanked the Guru and took Lalu and Maya with him to the moneylender. He must get money for their food on the way, and for tickets for the journey home, so that they might leave quickly while the moon was still favorable.

The moneylender lived in a real house, not in a clay hut without a chimney such as they lived in themselves. There were several rooms in the house, with doors between, and above one of them stood the word OFFICE. Lalu could not read, but he knew that the grand letters meant OFFICE because he had been with his father before when he had come to borrow money for seed corn.

The moneylender was a very fat man who puffed and

wheezed when he walked. Today he was sitting down, not in the room behind the door marked OFFICE, but out in the yard in the shadow of an acacia tree. He was fanning himself with a big fan and greeted them in a friendly manner. The moneylender was always friendly toward his clients until they began to discuss business.

The three of them had just put the tips of their fingers together and were saying "Salaam, Sahib!" when Kanga came rushing into the yard. She jumped up on Lalu, whining with delight and drowning out the polite greetings with her ear-splitting barks. She was dragging a broken string from her collar, and in her joy at having gained her freedom, she had rolled herself in manure and gave off a terrible smell.

"Kanga!" shouted Lalu, ashamed. He felt certain that it would be much more difficult to borrow money with a dog hanging around than without one, and worst of all a dog that smelled. Their father realized the same thing. He began to make many excuses, but no one heard him, because Kanga in her joy was making such a noise. Finally Lalu quieted her down, and Maya took hold of her collar and dragged her away from the moneylender.

But the moneylender was in a good humor that morning.

"What a lovely daughter you have, my good friend, Kumar Nagh!" he said, pointing at Maya in a patronizing way. "I really believe that she has blue eyes! So rare in North India! Come here, child! Can you dance for me? I'll hold the dog."

Unwillingly, Maya came nearer and handed Kanga's rope to him, but the moneylender let it go as if he had been burned.

"Ugh! What a stink! Get away, you dirty mongrel!" He laughed loudly and waved Kanga away with both his hands.

Kanga, who hated being on the leash, ran as far away across the yard as she could and lay down in the shadow, smell and all. Lalu gave a sigh of relief. The great man was not offended.

"Well, dance," said the moneylender. "Surely your mother has taught you to dance and sing the holy stories?"

"Yes," said Maya unhappily, because she did not at all want to dance for the moneylender. But when her father gave her a stern look, she tossed her braids back over her shoulders, lifted her brown arms above her head, and began obediently to dance. She danced and sang a story about Chaya, the goddess of shade and mercy, who sends rain to the dry earth and sleep to tired people.

"Lovely!" said the moneylender. "She dances beautifully and she is very pretty! You will not have to borrow a lot of money for her dowry when the time comes for her to get married."

"Alas," said the father, "I doubt whether I shall get her married. She has bad eyesight, and it is for that reason I have come to you now."

"And your boy is also a fine lad, strong and wiry. What have you come for, did you say?"

The father stated his difficult errand as best he could. It was bad enough to have to borrow money for seed corn, but that was nothing compared to borrowing for such an uncertain adventure as this.

"To Agra, did you say?" The moneylender scratched his chin. "Do you intend to send the girl on foot to Agra? Why, that is madness."

The father bent his head and looked as if he agreed.

"I am an ignorant man, Sahib," he said, excusing himself. "But I am told there is a hospital in Agra where they cure sick eyes. A hospital with the best doctors in the whole of India. And we have been to the Guru who says that as the moon is in its present phase . . ."

"You must not throw your money away in superstition, my good Kumar Nagh," said the moneylender sternly. "And all the way to Agra too! That will not be a cheap trip."

"I am an ignorant man, Sahib, but I had thought that the children could walk there, for they are strong and healthy, and then take the train home. Fifteen rupees . . ."

"Fifteen rupees! And you a poor man! You cannot pay me back before the rice is harvested and sold. It would be at least nineteen rupees with the interest."

Lalu was terrified when he heard how much money a trip to Agra would cost. He pulled at his father's arm.

"We can walk home also, Father . . ."

His father shook his head:

"Not both ways, the Guru said. A misfortune might befall you if we do not do exactly as he says. Remember that after the rainy season the road is infested with snakes, both kraits and cobras."

While their father and the moneylender were arguing about the money, Kanga had begun a voyage of discovery around the big yard and had slipped unseen into the house, tempted by good and unfamiliar smells. Lalu suddenly saw her tail disappearing through the door.

He left all further discussions about money to his father and the moneylender and rushed after the dog.

"Kanga! Come here. Come here at once! Kanga!"

But Kanga had suddenly become both deaf and blind. The only thing she thought of was the lovely smell of newly-ground meal.

Lalu jumped over the threshold of the open door and entered a large, sparsely furnished room with many rugs and cushions on the floor. This must be where the moneylender and his family spent the midday rest hour. An electric fan hummed in a corner, and on the table lay a red silk sari together with some ornaments that glittered brightly.

"Kanga! Where are you, Kanga?"

Kanga was nowhere to be seen, but in a corner stood a little box and it was speaking with a human voice.

Lalu knew well what it was, for there had been much talk about it. The moneylender was the only man in the village who owned such a new-fashioned thing. But it was the first time in his life that Lalu had ever actually seen or heard a radio. Fascinated, he stood still, forgetting where he was, forgetting Kanga.

The box was talking straight out into the empty air. No one was listening to it except himself. The words that came out were loud and clear.

"This is the World Health Organization speaking," said the box, but Lalu couldn't understand the long, strange words, even though they were in Hindi, his own language. "The World Health Organization has given a further grant of one million rupees for the treatment of lepers. It is now working in the villages of the vicinity, together with India's Ministry of Health . . ."

Lepers. He knew that word at any rate. The lepers sat apart on the station steps and were not allowed to come near the other beggars.

"There is therefore hope in the future for the lepers of India . . ."

Future? Could this box look into the future, just like the Guru?

Lalu touched the wireless set carefully. In front of it was a piece of soft material which moved weakly beneath his fingers, as if a living creature were breathing behind it.

The voice in the box continued to speak:

"Dr. Herman Singh states that . . ."

But Lalu never heard what the doctor in the radio stated. Furious shouts from the room next door yanked him quickly out of his dreams.

Kanga? What had happened to Kanga? What was she doing?

Suddenly Kanga rushed in with meal on her nose and her tail between her legs. And behind her came Akvi, the moneylender's large, angry wife. She filled the whole doorway with her big, thick body, and she had soft hanging cheeks that shook. Everything about Akvi was soft, both her body and her face, everything except her voice.

"You dirty village dog," she shouted, "eating my flour . . ."

But the mild voice in the radio was not, strangely enough, frightened by Akvi. It continued as if it were alone in the room:

"Cars with doctors and nurses will visit the villages daily. Many nations are cooperating in this tremendous effort . . ."

"May you fall dead!" Akvi shouted at Kanga, without paying any attention to the radio. But she forgot Kanga when she saw Lalu.

"Aha! Someone else has slipped into the house! What are you doing here . . . you . . . ?"

"Salaam, Memsahib!" said Lalu, and bowed, for he had better manners than the angry Akvi.

"India's new Five Year Plan," said the polite radio voice, "will change the whole future of the suffering Indian people . . ."

"I'll give you suffering Indian people . . ." Akvi took hold of Lalu and shook him till he thought his arms and legs would be wrenched out of joint. The table with the red silk sari danced before his eyes. Akvi's hands were not as soft as they looked.

"Who are you? Answer me!"

She shook him again so violently that the words with which he was going to answer her questions swung to and fro in a jumble in his head. It was with some difficulty that he fished out the names he needed.

"I am Lalu, the son of Kumar Nagh."

"Your mother's sorrow!" She let him go, and Lalu felt himself to make sure he was still in one piece.

"I am not my mother's sorrow," he said obstinately. For Lalu was a sensible boy and had not yet learned to be afraid of moneylenders and their wives.

"Are you answering me back? What are you doing here anyway, you little thief and rascal?"

"I am not a thief," said Lalu. But he felt a little more unsure of himself, for it was only too obvious that Kanga at least had been stealing. "I only came in to fetch the dog."

"Out you go. And take the dog with you. She's stinking."

Lalu caught hold of Kanga's collar and edged himself backwards out of the room, so that he might not turn his back on his enemy. But Kanga turned her head toward the newly-ground flour in the side room and behaved as if she had never been in polite society before. Akvi seized a stick standing against a wall and lunged across the floor to chase Kanga out, but she was so angry that she stumbled on one of her own rugs. She reached for the edge of the table to save herself, but only caught hold of the red silk sari and dragged both it and the ornaments down with her in her fall. She was up almost as soon as she was down, and shrieked: "You rascally little wretch! This is all your fault!" She was very angry now.

Lalu made a quick escape.

Still scolding, Akvi went back to her spoiled flour.

When Lalu got out into the yard his father had managed to reduce the interest a good deal, and had obtained fourteen precious rupees for the journey. Bowing low, he thanked the moneylender and returned home relieved with Lalu, Maya and the stinking Kanga.

A little way from the house they met Kamak's uncle. He was singing with joy on his way to the moneylender to borrow money for seed corn. His time of begging was at an end.

But when they asked him how he managed to get into the hospital, the words he spoke were as puzzling as Akvi's radio. They were all about India's Five Year Plan, and the doctors in Agra, all jumbled together. But he made one thing very clear. Whatever happened, Maya must get to Agra. Real miracles were performed there.

4

WHAT HAPPENED IN
ALLAHABAD

Maya and Lalu went out into the cattle shed to say goodby to the buffaloes, who were standing in the half darkness, dragging at their chains. They were playful as Indian house buffaloes often are and bent down their foreheads to the children so that they might be scratched between the horns. Then they bellowed at them in their deep, warm voices.

"Oh dear. They know that we are going away," said Maya.

Lalu swung himself up onto the neck of Kasha, the largest of the buffaloes.

"Dear old Kasha! Who will ride you to the water in the morning when I am gone? And who'll drag hay for you from the stack? There'll only be the little ones now. Poor old Kasha."

Maya went from one to the other, stroking their necks.

"How long are we going to be away, Lalu?"

Lalu shrugged his shoulders.

"How can I tell? A long time, I'm certain."

Maya sighed. "We'll walk as quickly as we can, Kasha!"

The buffaloes bellowed after them when they went.

Their two small brothers tagged along after them everywhere. Lalu and Maya were going far, far away, and this transformed them from being Lalu and Maya into strange, almost grown-up beings. The little boys looked at them with serious eyes, hung around them and said goodbye to all the animals, just as if they too were going away.

Surmi was standing out in the shade of the house wall. They must say goodbye to him too. Surmi was to have gone with them, but like the cautious animal he was, he had begun to limp so that they had to give up that idea. A lame donkey is not much good, and when Lalu stroked his neck he knew that he would never see him again. Surmi looked as if he knew it too.

"You are stubborn, old donkey, and I've often been angry with you. But still there is no one, no one, like old Surmi," whispered Lalu into the shaggy animal's ear. "Never again will you throw me off into the nettles, you darling old Surmi."

Next came Kanga's turn, and saying goodbye to her was the hardest of all. Lalu had begged and prayed to be allowed to take her with them, but his father had been adamant.

Kanga stood tied to a pole in the middle of the yard, and if there was anything that Kanga hated it was to be tethered like a buffalo. She stood on tiptoe stroking Lalu with her front paws, beseeching him with her large, sad eyes.

"You cannot come either, Kanga. Father will not allow it. Father says that it will be difficult enough for Maya and me to feed ourselves on such a long journey, and it would be madness to have to feed a dog, too. You understand that?"

Kanga whined but only understood that she was tied up while Lalu was free.

"You would not like to starve, would you, Kanga?" Lalu comforted her. But he did not really believe that Kanga would ever starve to death. She was always all over the place and would be sure to find something to eat, with her sharp nose.

He freed himself from the dog and asked his father once more.

"Kanga could help us, Father. She would warn us of snakes and chase away the jackals."

"Snakes? Jackals? But you must not take a single step off the highroad, son! You must stay close to other people and keep to the road, as I told you. And that food that you get must not be shared with a dog."

Lalu bent his head and turned away.

Maya whispered to him:

"Kanga will follow us the moment she is loose. She has a better scent that any other dog in the neighborhood."

Lalu shook his head:

"We're going to drive the first part of the road, Maya, so how will she be able to find her way after us?"

Their mother rolled their sleeping mats around the food which consisted of a big bundle of rice, some dried fish, bread and ghee. She also packed their wooden bowls, a tiny saucepan and a couple of thin woolen cloths to keep Lalu and Maya warm at night. Nani wrapped a sweet cake in banana leaves and included it in the bundle.

"If you eat all this carefully and with common sense it will last you a long while," said their mother.

"Yes, Mother," said Lalu.

"Keep your eyes open and your mouths shut and I am sure all will go well with you," said Nani. "And if you get ill chew betel leaves which will act as a fever cure."

"Yes, Nani."

Their father repeated what he had said to them already at least ten times:

"As soon as you get to Agra, Lalu, go to your grand-uncle, Kadri Ali Singh, as quickly as you can. He is a servant in the household of Ali Raza. Now mind you, don't forget their names!"

"No, Father."

The neighbor's ox wagon now came, creaking along with its large, spreading load of hay held in place by a bamboo pole. In front of the cart sat the driver swinging his ox whip. The children climbed up while Kanga howled and pulled in vain against the rope which held her fast. The wagon jerked forward. The long journey had begun.

Their mother stood with the youngest child on her hip, waving to them. Nani swung her red head scarf. Their father stood there, looking very serious and holding a little brother by each hand. He did not move.

It had been bad enough saying goodbye to the animals, but it was much more painful to leave their parents and brothers standing by the roadside while they themselves drove away. Lalu felt as if he were a branch pulled roughly away from the parent trunk, a branch which must certainly wither. He experienced a strange sinking feeling in the pit of his stomach. Why was his father standing so still without waving? Why did he look so sad?

Maya sat happily on the hay, not at all like a broken-off branch. In her new, shining red tunic she looked much more like a ripe raspberry. To her, Lalu was the most important member of the family. All was well as long as he was there.

Dusk fell quickly as it always does in India, wiping out the houses and the people in the village. They were to drive the entire night in order to reach Allahabad by morning. Lalu turned around and opened his shirt to the evening breeze. There was still light over the fields, but under the trees where they were driving it was almost dark. A storm lantern hung beneath the load of hay, throwing a ring of light in front of the legs of the oxen. There was not much traffic, no hooting cars, just a few other ox wagons on their way to market. Grasshoppers sang in the cactus growth along the road. The moon was rising and Lalu lay awake for a long time looking at it.

When they woke the next morning, the sun was rising behind a thick row of banana trees, coloring half the sky red. Allahabad was just coming into view, its crowded houses and golden temples gleaming in the rising sun.

The driver, who had been asleep as he sat at the front of the wagon, now woke up. He had allowed the oxen to follow the other wagons. A little later he stopped by an irrigation canal which lay glittering in a green field. He took the yoke off the oxen and let them drink.

Many people were lined up in front of them along the canal. They washed themselves and said their morning prayers. Maya shivered sleepily in the cold morning while she washed herself, although the water in the canal was warmer than the air. They could not take a long rest for the driver was anxious to get on, so they just had time to swallow a little rice before moving ahead again.

Ox wagons laden with goods for the market were entering the highway from all the side roads. Shouting, fighting boys drove flocks of bleating goats and lowing buffaloes which raised huge clouds of dust, while the stream of pedestrians, cyclists and drivers grew constantly thicker. Lalu and Maya had never seen so many people and cattle before.

They had to get off the wagon at the city gates. Rows of ox wagons with provisions of all sorts stood there waiting to pay the market dues. Maya and Lalu thanked the neighbor politely for letting them ride with him, took up their bundles, and walked away into the crowd. From now on there would be no more moving forward while resting on a fragrant pile of hay.

Scarcely had they got down from the wagon and begun to walk before Lalu noticed that Maya was carrying a cloth bag. He knew very well what was in it. It contained all Maya's small white stones and colored pieces of glass which she loved to play with by making them into patterns. She had not been able to leave them behind her.

"Maya," said Lalu sternly, "we can't drag those stones all the way to Agra. Empty the bag."

But Maya would not do so. She insisted on holding on
to her treasures and stamped her bare foot on the pave-
ment until her ankle rings clattered.

"I'll carry them myself. My bag has nothing to do with
you."

"But you won't even have time to play with them,
Maya. We have to walk, walk, walk. And besides, we've
plenty to carry without them."

Maya at length agreed to throw away the biggest and
heaviest of her treasures, only keeping the smallest and
most colorful. She buried them under a bush, and turned
around more than once to look back at the place where
she had left them.

It was no light task to make their way through the
town on market day, and they soon realized the difference between walking and driving. They were shoved
here and pushed there and Lalu had to hold Maya's thin
little hand tightly in his own. The stream of animals and
people seemed to close around them until they thought
they would be squashed to death. The noise was deafening.

Lalu tried to learn the way to Agra, but people only
laughed and shook their heads. Somebody pointed
vaguely in a direction beyond the crowd of people.

"We'll be trampled down in this crowd," Lalu shouted
to Maya. "We must turn around and get out of it!"

But to turn was easier said than done. The streets were
no longer so tightly packed, but everybody was going

in the same direction and nothing could be done except
to follow the crowd.

A holy cow with large gilded horns came along the
street, walking slowly and with great dignity against the
stream. People turned aside in front of her to let her
pass, and a man in uniform suddenly and unintentionally
stepped on one of Maya's bare feet with his heavy boot.

She shrieked.

"I want to get away," she wept. "It's hurting. It's hurting terribly! Take me away, Lalu!"

Lalu turned resolutely around, fixed his eyes on the
golden horns of the holy cow walking so calmly against
the crowd of pedestrians as if she were alone in the

world, and pushed his way behind her with the weeping
Maya clinging to him. Putting his bundle on his head, he
freed one hand, took hold of the cow's tail and hung on
to it until they were safely out of the worst of the crowd.
Then the cow suddenly decided to lie down in the middle of the traffic, which reverently drove around her.

Maya continued to cry.

"He had iron on his boot. Look, I'm bleeding!"

In the part of the street which lay in shadow, a long
row of shops stretched out, offering all sorts of food.
Lalu, dragging Maya with him, bought two annas' worth
of cooked soybeans, which were handed to him in a
banana leaf. Then they went up the steps of a golden
Hindu temple and sat down on the top one.

"Here you are—eat," said Lalu. "We'll try to keep
away from markets and people in the future."

The beans comforted Maya. She ate, examined her
trampled toes, and thought that perhaps she could still
move them.

"They *must* be all right, Maya. You've got to walk all
the way to Agra on them."

"They *can* walk to Agra," decided Maya, and wiped
the tears from her dirty face.

While they sat there on the temple steps, something
suddenly happened which made the journey more difficult for them than it need have been.

Directly across the street from the place where they
were sitting lay the town prison. A policeman in khaki
uniform and shorts stood outside it shouting a number of

inquiries and notices through a loud-speaker. It was the first time the two little travelers had ever come across a thing that could turn the voice of a man into the trumpeting of an elephant, and they could not take their eyes off the man and the loud-speaker.

"The police are looking for Lalu and Maya Kumar Nagh, thirteen and seven years old," roared the voice. "Lalu is dark and is wearing a shirt with a brown and black pattern. Maya has a red tunic and long, green cotton trousers. She has blue eyes."

There they sat on the temple steps and heard their own names thundered across the square. Maya stopped chewing and listened with open mouth.

"Did you hear that, Lalu? He said Maya and Lalu."

"A shirt with a black and brown pattern and a red tunic—that's what we're wearing."

They looked at each other.

"A reward of one hundred rupees is promised for any information that will lead to the capture of Lalu and Maya Kumar Nagh," shouted the voice. "I repeat: they are thirteen and seven years old, and are wearing a shirt with a black and brown pattern, and a red tunic and green trousers. The seven-year-old girl has blue eyes."

"Is it Father wanting us back?" wondered Maya.

"Father doesn't have a hundred rupees to pay for us."

"Let's go and ask!" Maya slipped down the steps, but Lalu took hold of her braids and kept her back.

"Then you will never get to Agra!"

Maya pulled herself up again. "Can't you see, idiot,

that if it were Father calling us he would have asked us to go home. It is the police who want to get hold of us! The police!"

The policeman repeated the notice, and the names thundered over their heads.

"A hundred rupees promised in reward!"

People began to look at them. Lalu quickly swept the last soya beans into the banana leaf and tightened his fingers around it.

"We must be going, Maya."

He stowed away the beans under his shirt, caught up the two bundles, took Maya's arm, and led her in a run down the steps. They ran as fast as they could. Maya knocked against people, was scolded, and stumbled on. Voices bellowed behind their backs as they ran.

The crowds lessened, but they did not dare turn around and look behind them. They just ran, through the city gates, and away along the highroad. Only then did they realize that they were running in the wrong direction and were going homeward.

Tired out, they sank down in the shadow of a tree.

"Let's get home quickly, Lalu, before the police catch us!"

"We haven't done anything wrong," said Lalu obstinately, and pulled off the tell-tale shirt. "I'm going to get to Agra, even if I have to go there naked!" Angrily he put his shirt into his bundle, and turning to Maya he said: "You must not look at people, or they will see your eyes are blue."

"I want to go home," said Maya. "I can't look only at the ground all the way from here to Agra." She cried for the third time that day. "I want to go home, do you hear, Lalu! I want to go home!"

Suddenly an animal jumped up on Lalu. Neither of them had seen where it came from, but it was a dusty, breathless animal, which licked Lalu's ear and whined with joy. It was Kanga!

Lalu threw both arms around the dog with a joy almost as great as hers.

"Kanga! You wonderful Kanga! But however have you found us? We rode!"

He pulled the dog down onto his knees and patted her back.

"I knew you had a very fine nose, Kanga. But we did not walk!"

Maya had stopped crying and was dancing around them.

"I hung my scarf down from the wagon so that it touched the ground," she laughed. "Didn't you see how dirty it was?"

"But why didn't you tell me?"

"You would have been so disappointed if Kanga had not come."

Lalu laughed and shook his head. That was the thing about Maya. She went around in her half darkness and thought of wonderful ideas that never occurred to other people.

Maya stroked Kanga's dusty coat.

"I'm sure it's a good omen that Kanga has found us, Lalu."

Whether it was a good omen or not, Lalu did not know, but at any rate it made them forget the loud and horrible voice of the policeman. They were now outside the busy city and were able to ask and find the right road to Agra. Maya was still limping a little from the accident, but they walked on without stopping until the fierce noonday heat made them halt. By then Allahabad lay far behind them, with its prison and its loud-speaker. They ate, and slept for four hours in the shade of a palm tree.

5

JHANDU, THE CAMEL DRIVER

The evening breeze had spung up when they started their journey again, and the traffic increased as it grew cooler. Cars and bicycles rushed past them. Camels, donkeys and oxen walked along the road with slow steps. Thin horses clopped along, pulling loaded tongas.

Lalu and Maya, followed by Kanga, walked along the side of the road, which was covered with dry dust. The sinking sun fell on the yellow mustard fields and on hedges of sugar cane and billowing wheat fields, stretching as far as the eye could see. The narrow irrigation canals shone like silver bands where they ran between the fields. From time to time they passed through a village of gray mud huts, crowed with dark-eyed, half-naked youngsters. At these times they walked faster and kept apart from each other. Their fear of the loud-speaker in the temple square was still with them. Who wouldn't want to earn one hundred rupees by reporting a boy with a patterned shirt and a girl with blue eyes?

Darkness fell and only then did they dare walk together again.

Maya still limped.

At first Lalu pretended he did not notice it, hoping that her foot would get better as they went on, but instead she seemed to limp even more. She did not say very much but walked with her head a little to one side, dragging her foot behind her.

How was he going to get her all the way to Agra when she was limping right at the very start?

He stopped once or twice and thumbed a passing car in the vain hope that it would stop, but the drivers paid no attention to him.

He was accustomed to this. There are too many children in India who stand by the side of the roads, trying to thumb a ride in the cars that pass. Why should the drivers single him out above all the others?

Maya continued to limp. Lalu plucked up enough courage to ask a mule driver if he would give her a little lift, but the driver refused. In India there are some people who belong to a high caste and some to a lower one. Those who belong to a high caste are looked up to, but those who belong to the lower castes are thought to be of little importance. Lalu and Maya did not belong to a high caste, and there was nothing to be done about it. The mule driver turned his back on them and did not answer, so that was the end of that.

Nobody noticed the children, nobody bothered about them, but Lalu would not give up so soon. Close to a village where the families were sitting around the fires, singing in the darkness, stood a solitary camel. He was clearly outlined against the evening sky, ready for travel, with his head turned westward toward Agra. He already had a heavy bundle of hemp on his back and his owner was in the process of adding another to the load.

Lalu realized that unless Maya was given a lift they would have to stop and wait until her foot was better, and no one could tell how long that would be. They might even have to give up the whole journey. He decided to ask the camel driver if Maya might sit up there on the camel, as she had hurt her foot.

The camel driver was a small, insignificant-looking man, with a loud voice. He glanced up at them from beneath eyebrows so large and bushy they looked almost like a beard.

"Are you wandering along the highroad begging?" he asked.

"We are not beggars, we are travelers," said Lalu.

The camel driver bent down over Maya.

"You have blue eyes," he said.

Maya pulled herself away and her hands fumbled for Lalu. She was forever forgetting to keep her eyes fixed on the ground! She would never get away from her wretched blue eyes.

"I once had a little girl who had blue eyes," thundered

the camel driver. "But she was too wise to grow up. How have you hurt your foot?" he asked.

Without waiting for an answer, he picked up Maya and settled her comfortably on top of the camel's load.

"You will be all right up there," he reassured her. "You can go to sleep if you wish."

It all happened so quickly and unexpectedly they could find no words with which to thank him, and they started off almost immediately.

Maya pitched and tossed on the top of the camel's load, high above all cars, bicycles and people down on the dusty road. Her foot ceased to ache as soon as she rested it. But after a while the pitching made her feel seasick, and she began to cry a little. Then the camel driver told her to lie flat on her face on the hemp and she soon fell asleep.

Lalu caught hold of a piece of rope hanging down the side of the camel and clung to it as best he could. All went well. He felt he could walk to the end of the world now that Maya was no longer limping along beside him. This was the best thing that could possibly have happened to them. Her foot was resting and they were still able to continue their journey without a pause.

It grew darker and darker and hundreds of frogs croaked in the canals on either side of the road. There was no light except from the headlights of passing cars and as the night wore on these became fewer and fewer. At last, they only met one or two heavily-loaded mules or an ox wagon or two. Sometimes a shadowy jackal scuttled across the road, stopped suddenly and looked at them with shining eyes before it disappeared. Then Kanga growled a little and rubbed her wet nose against Lalu's bare legs.

Lalu and the camel driver walked on silently, separated from each other by the large beast. Lalu could hear the camel driver muttering to himself now and then as he walked along, but whether it was to keep himself awake or because he was upset about something, Lalu could not guess. He learned nothing about either the camel or its master. The camel kicked out at Lalu if he got behind it, but Maya was happy on its back, and the man, although he sounded cross, was kind, much kinder than any of the grand car owners.

It was Lalu's first night of walking on the highway, but the camel driver did not seem inclined to rest. Lalu managed to keep on his feet by holding onto the rope and only stumbled now and again. Never in all his life had he been so tired. At last dawn broke over the misty fields. Lalu turned his sleepy face upward and saw how the stars grew smaller and smaller until they faded away altogether and disappeared.

Then at last the camel driver stopped by a well. The camel knelt down and Lalu helped to unload the bales. They all washed and said their morning prayers, the camel driver turning toward the rising sun with closed eyes and folded hands. Afterward they settled themselves down on the edge of a wheat field to eat and warm themselves in the morning sun. Maya was shivering from the cold night air and morning hunger, and Lalu had to rub her back and arms. The camel driver, Jhandu, as he called himself, threw a woolen blanket over to her and Lalu wrapped her up in it. In the meantime Jhandu built a little fire of dried camel droppings which he had brought with him in a sack. Then he gave them tea sweetened with honey and hard bread and wild figs. There was enough for them all, even for Kanga.

"Eat," he said. "Shy hands never make a fat body. There's plenty here."

Their strength returned with the good food. Lalu swallowed the hot tea, looking over the edge of his cup at Jhandu's thin cheeks and hollow chest; surely he needed the food himself.

"Do you like traveling back and forth with a camel?" he asked.

"I hate it," said Jhandu, as calmly as if he were talking about the weather.

"Why?"

"Your questions are more stupid than most people's," said Jhandu.

But later he explained that he had pawned his property during the year of famine and now he must work day and night in order to make enough to buy it back.

After they had finished eating, Jhandu put some healing ointment on Maya's foot and bound it up with a stiff cloth which, he said, would support it. Then he asked how far she had to go with the bad foot.

"To Agra," said Lalu.

"To Agra? As far as all that?" Jhandu lifted his bushy eyebrows with astonishment. "All the way alone?"

"Yes. We must do the best we can by ourselves."

"Well, better alone than in bad company, as the old proverb says. What are you going to do in Agra?"

"We're going to the hospital so that Maya's eyes can be cured."

"The hospital? There is never any room in the hospital.

My little girl died because there was no room for her in the hospital."

"There must be room," said Lalu.

Then he told Jhandu all about how Maya had been given a place in the school but would lose it if her eyes did not get better.

"Besides, I have need of her eyes," said Lalu, "for I intend to learn to read at the same time as she does."

He had expected Jhandu to praise him for his wish to learn to read, but he was disappointed.

"Indeed. So it is for your own sake that you are dragging this poor little girl across half of India," Jhandu thundered. "Not for her own sake?"

"For Maya's sake too, and mostly for her, so that she may not go blind."

"If you do it for her sake, it is an honorable journey and God will help you," said Jhandu harshly. "If it is for your own sake, it is a foolhardy journey and God will not help you. There is no room for profit and honor on the same plate."

"What is profit?" asked Maya.

"Your own advantage," answered Jhandu.

Lalu made no answer to this. He had never liked moral sermons.

The three of them went along together, walking at night and sleeping in the heat of the noonday sun. Although camels are slower than some other animals, the children got much further than they would have otherwise. Jhandu told them many stories and adventures as they walked, but the story they remembered best was the one about the silver money in the fireplace:

"There was once a poor farmer," Jhandu said one day, as they lay in the shade resting, "who used to plow his fields, sow his seed and reap his harvest year in and year out. But after working hard for years he was just as poor as the day he started. One morning, when he knelt down to say his morning prayers, he shouted:

" 'Merciful god Siva! Give me money to pay my debts! If I am ever to get riches in this hard life it must come from you. You who can do what you will, put the money here in the fireplace so that I can pay my debts.'

"After he had prayed, he rose and went out into the fields with the oxen to plow. Now it happened that as he walked over the rough land, he tore his clothes on a cactus plant. He was very angry, and swearing that it should not happen again, he dug the ground around the plant and pulled it up by its root. Suddenly down in the hole he saw the edge of a buried clay pot. Very excited, he dug down further until he was able to lift the lid off the pot. It was filled to the brim with silver money. At first he was beside himself with joy, but then he became thoughtful and said:

" 'O good god Siva, I asked you to put the money in the fireplace so that I might pay my debts. If you had listened to my prayer you would have put it there and not under a cactus plant in an unplowed field. This is not my money.'

"He left the treasure lying where he had found it,

drove his oxen home and told his wife, whose name was Drushka, about his strange find in the field.

" 'Somebody or other has left it there and will come back some day to fetch it. I cannot take other people's money.'

"Drushka thought her husband was foolish, and was very angry with him, and went off to a neighbor while he slept.

" 'That stupid husband of mine found a lot of money under a cactus plant in the field, but he says it is not the god's intention that he should take it. Go out, fetch it for yourself and give half of it to me!' said Drushka.

"The neighbor was very pleased at the suggestion and went out to the field where he found the cactus plant that had been dug up and the pot beneath it, but when he opened the pot it was full of poisonous snakes.

"Then the man thought:

" 'Drushka is my enemy. She wants to kill me so she has fooled me into taking the lid off a pot that is full of snakes.'

"So he fastened the lid down tightly again and carried the pot home and when darkness fell he went up onto his neighbor's roof and emptied the snakes from the pot down the chimney, for all this happened up in the north where people have chimneys in their houses.

"At dawn, when the poor farmer knelt to say his morning prayer, the sunshine fell onto the fireplace and revealed a pile of glittering silver money.

"Then tears of joy ran down the farmer's cheeks and he thanked the good god Siva:

" 'Gratitude and praise be thine, O generous god! Now I know that the money is mine because you have put it on the hearth as I asked you.' "

"He was a pious man, but if I had been he, I would have taken the money when I found it in the field," said the practical Lalu.

"Then perhaps you would have had no joy from it," said Jhandu. "It is not enough just to have money. You also must have a blessing with it."

That anything but blessing could come with such a thing as money was quite beyond Lalu's understanding, and he had had so many sermons in his life that he heartily disliked them.

The children had two calm, secure days of travel with Jhandu and his camel. No one noticed Maya, who was almost hidden in all the hemp on the camel's back, and Lalu dared to put on his shirt when the sun became too hot for his back. But on the third day something frightening happened.

Just as Jhandu and Lalu were looking around for a sheltered spot in which to sleep during the heat of the noonday sun, a motorcycle stopped behind them. Lalu turned around quickly and looked straight into the eyes of the khaki-clad policeman from the Temple Square in Allahabad.

The man gazed at Lalu's brown and black patterned

shirt, and then looked around for Maya without seeing her.

"How old are you?" he asked Lalu, taking him by the arm.

"Th—thirteen," answered Lalu, too surprised to be able to think up a new age for himself.

The policeman shifted his inquiring eyes to Kanga and seemed to be disappointed that she had neither blue eyes nor green trousers.

"Have you a sister?" He gripped Lalu's arm harder than ever but Lalu had now recovered enough to shake his head.

Jhandu came over to them. "Has this boy a sister?" repeated the policeman.

"A sister? What would he be doing with a sister?" asked Jhandu.

"I am hunting for two children who are wanted by the police. Thirteen and seven. I have been riding up and down this road for three days now, for I know they cannot have gone very far away. They are wanted for theft."

"Theft?" Lalu could not believe his own ears.

"What have they stolen?" asked Jhandu.

"They are a pack of thieves."

Some half-smothered sounds came from high up on the camel's back, but the policeman heard neither them nor Lalu's thumping heart.

"There is a reward of a hundred rupees for catching

the little thieves," he said. "They are thirteen and seven years old. Have you seen them?"

"A hundred rupees. That is a lot of money," said Jhandu.

"Of course it's a lot of money. But I have no more time to run around looking for runaway children."

"Thirteen and seven year olds have stolen goods worth a hundred rupees?" said Jhandu. "That does not sound very likely. How could such little children have stolen so much?"

"They have, I assure you. There are such children about everywhere. But I will give you half of it if you will get hold of them for me. Fifty rupees."

"Fifty rupees," said Jhandu. "That would mean that I could buy back my land. Especially if I sold the camel, too."

"The seven-year-old girl has blue eyes, a red blouse and green trousers. The boy is wearing a brown and black patterned shirt."

"Just like this one here?" asked Jhandu, pointing at Lalu.

Lalu felt his legs give way under him. "Now he is going to hand us over," he thought. "He'll drag Maya down from the camel in another minute because he wants to buy his land back."

"Yes. But this one has no sister. Only a dog. There is nothing about dogs in the announcement. Perhaps it is your dog?"

"No," said Jhandu.

Lalu was held so tightly by the policeman that he could not move. "We are lost," he thought. "Jhandu wants his land back and what could be more reasonable than that?"

"The whole place is full of boys wearing brown and black shirts," said the policeman, "but have you seen a girl?"

"A hundred rupees is a lot of money," said Jhandu. "If I were you I would turn my motorcycle around and hunt in all the villages. It is useless to go on any further. A seven year old could never have walked as far as this."

"Not unless she has been given a lift."

"No one gives lifts to beggars and thieves," said Jhandu, and again Lalu thought he heard a little sound from the top of the camel's back.

"You are right, they may be hiding in a village," said the policeman. He let Lalu go and began to start up his motorcycle. A moment later he had disappeared in a cloud of dust.

"That money did not lie on my hearth," said Jhandu, looking at Lalu.

"No," said Lalu weakly. He had to sit down right in the middle of the road because his legs would hold him up no longer.

Maya climbed down from the camel's back. She was not pale like Lalu, but red with fury.

"We are not thieves," she shouted. "We have never taken as much as an anna. We are not thieves."

"That is just what I was going to ask you," said Jhandu, "and I believe you. You don't look as if you have much money, either stolen or not stolen."

"I can't imagine why they think so," said Lalu from the dust of the road.

"Children and the poor are blamed for everything," said Jhandu, "and you are both."

The same day, after the midday rest, they said good-bye to Jhandu. He was going no further and they had to go on without him.

Maya cried and Jhandu comforted her. "Your foot is just as good as Lalu's now, and he who has no horse must ride on his own feet. You will get on all right. I am sorry that we cannot keep each other company any longer. I'd like to have Lalu's strong arm to depend on when the bales have to be lifted on and off."

Lalu pulled out his money and wanted to pay for the ride and their food, but Jhandu quickly put himself between Lalu and the traffic.

"You are really the most stupid boy I have ever met. Imagine pulling out your money here in the middle of the road. You ought to know that people cannot bear the sight of money without wanting to take it. Hide it away as quickly as you can."

He threw his woolen shawl over his thin shoulders and swung the camel around into a side road. The two children remained standing there looking after him as long as they could see him, the small thin man beside the tall camel.

They never saw him again, and their life on the high-road became much more difficult after they parted from Jhandu.

6

IN A BAOLI

Now that Maya's foot was healed, Lalu thought that they would be able to go farther in a day than they had with the camel, but he soon realized that a seven year old does not find it as easy to turn night into day as a thirteen year old. It was easy enough to sleep in the day, but when it came to walking at night, well, that was more difficult. Lalu realized at last that he must let Maya spread out her sleeping mat and get a few hours' sleep at night as well as in the day. Gradually he gave up asking people how far it was to Agra.

They had both learned a great deal from Jhandu: how to find safe places in which to rest; how to wash in the canals; how to make fires with sun-dried buffalo dung which they collected during the day, and on which they cooked their rice in the tiny saucepan that Lalu had packed in his bundle. Mixed with ghee, the rice was quite satisfying and filled their stomachs, but Maya often grew tired, and then Lalu had to tell her all the stories and adventures he could remember in order to get her going again.

Three days after Jhandu had left them, they came upon a baoli. A baoli is an underground hiding place where there is a well. They were built a long time ago by people who sought shelter in warlike times.

Lalu and Maya had ventured onto pasture land to collect manure, and were walking along a bamboo hedge. It was there that they found it. Heavy cactus growth hid the entrance and they only discovered it when Maya took a wrong step and stumbled onto the hidden stone stairs which led down to the well. Lalu was standing on top of the baoli itself without having discovered it, so well was it hidden.

They realized at once that this was a real baoli. Air channels and hidden light holes made it possible to see and breathe down in it, and it was very cool.

They stood in it, looking around at the thick plastered walls, the sand on the floor and the well in the corner.

"Just imagine if we found treasure down here," said Maya. "Gold coins, jewels . . ."

Lalu shook his head. "It must certainly have been plundered a long time ago."

But he, too, had heard stories about children who, while they were playing, had found old forgotten baolis in which were hidden wonderful treasures and costly jewels.

"Well," said Lalu, "perhaps we might find an old coin

or two down here. It's obvious no one's been here for a long time. Maybe we *are* the first people to discover it."

They began digging in the sand.

"You talk about finding coins," panted Maya. "No— a pearl as large as a dove's egg! That would be something to find! Or two pearls, one for mother and one for Nani."

Lalu was more sober.

"I'd be glad enough to find some gold coins so that I could buy an old second-hand bicycle and ride the rest of the way to Agra with you," he said.

They turned over every stone at the edge of the well and felt in the cracks which were everywhere in the plastered walls.

"It ought to be a diamond," said Maya. "A diamond that would make us rich for the rest of our lives."

She lifted up a handful of sand and peered at it in her near-sighted way. "Or a ruby. I think I would like to find a ruby best of all." She passed her sensitive fingers all over the place, both high and low. The time passed. They heard Kanga whining up on the stairs, but she would not come down into the baoli, and they were too busy hunting for treasure to go up and fetch her.

"Just a little topaz," said Maya, who now began to lessen her demands and transfer them to semi-precious stones. "Just enough to pay the moneylender."

But they found nothing. The little stones they threw down into the well struck the bottom with a bang that showed it was dry. Finally they went up again.

The heat beat against them and Kanga stopped whining and jumped up happily all over them.

"How stupid you are, Kanga," said Maya patting her. "What are you afraid of? You can't imagine how lovely it is down there even if there isn't any treasure."

Two goats were standing in the shadow of the bamboo hedge and gazed at the children with an unfriendly look in their eyes. There was not a breath of air.

"Lalu," begged Maya, "let us sleep down there for a bit. Then we can go on hunting when we are rested."

"It is too early in the day to rest," answered Lalu. "Besides, we should collect some more buffalo dung."

"Pearls are better than dung," said Maya, "and gold coins even better than pearls. With them we could buy cow dung."

"There are no pearls down there, you silly. I tell you, this baoli was plundered a long time ago."

"Just for a little while, Lalu!" She looked so defenseless standing there in the blazing sun. She was pale, too.

"Perhaps I am driving her too hard," thought Lalu. "What would I do if she fell ill in the middle of the high road? Then I'd never get her either to Agra or back home." At last he gave in.

They went down, unrolled their sleeping mats and spread them out on the sandy floor beside the empty well. But Kanga would not come down. Lalu had to go up and fetch her, but she struggled hard and had to be dragged down the steps by her collar. They ate a little

dried fish, gulped down some water from the water flask
and lay down to sleep. Kanga settled down eventually
and crawled up onto Maya's sleeping mat. Soon they
were all three fast asleep.

The sun went its hot way across a cloudless sky, the
dust lay thick on the highroad with its noise of bicycles
and cars, but down in the strange sleeping place where
the children lay it was quiet and cool, and they slept as
heavily as only tired children can. The color came back
into Maya's face as she lay stretched out on the sleeping
mat. Lalu ceased to be on guard down in this safe hiding
place and slept heavily, breathing deeply and restfully.
None of them realized that a large cobra had wriggled

up out of the empty well and was gliding past them at full length.

Lalu woke when Kanga whined. Still half asleep, he saw the hair on Kanga's back rising and a snake's head lifted high against the wall.

It was the first time in his life that he had been so near a living cobra. Fascinated, he stared at the almost human head which moved slowly backward and forward. Kanga, trembling like a leaf, whined softly.

Lalu did not dare even to lift his head for he knew the moment he moved the snake would strike. He dug his hands down into the sand, for in his sleep he had rolled off his mat and was lying on the bare ground.

How long he lay there, stiff as a stick, staring at the swaying thing, he did not know. He could not say whether it was a minute or an hour. The snake coiled its long body into a ring, and Lalu watched in terror as it quivered, sending ripples of motion along its entire length.

Suddenly Kanga's whining woke Maya and she jumped up innocently. Lalu let out one deafening shriek which echoed back and forth in the cave, and Kanga answered it with a deep, loud fit of barking that sounded more like a wolf than a dog.

Without really knowing what he was doing, Lalu grabbed up the sleeping mat and threw it over the snake's head, just as he had seen snake hunters do when they went hunting for snake skins during the rainy season. Then he gripped Maya's arm and they both rushed blindly up the high steps, with Lalu's shriek still lingering and echoing in the baoli behind them. Whether his sudden yell had frightened the cobra, or whether the snake was simply so old and tired that he could no longer move swiftly, Lalu did not know, nor had he time to think about it. When they reached the top, the two of them stood in the blazing sunshine, both of them shivering and trembling and pale with fright.

They did not know what to do now. They couldn't afford to leave their sleeping mats and food behind them, but they didn't dare to go down again to the baoli. No one escaped alive twice from a cobra.

With Maya half crying beside him, Lalu ran back to the highroad to try to get help. Something must be done. They stood almost directly in front of a fine car and signaled wildly for it to stop.

"A cobra," stammered Maya when the car drew to a sudden halt. "Help us! A cobra!"

A rich Indian gentleman was sitting at the wheel. "A cobra, here on the highroad?"

"No. In the hole over there. A baoli . . ."

"A baoli? A cobra? Do you think that I am going to go down into an old forsaken hole to catch a cobra? Get out of the way, children, I'm in a hurry. I must try to get to Agra today."

"Oh, take us with you," cried Lalu. "Please, please!"

The gentleman in the car was more surprised than angry.

"What are you going to do there?"

Lalu made a desperate attempt to tell their story to the busy man, but the man was impatient and started up the car before Lalu could finish. The boy's frantic explanations died away in the noise of the engine.

"Stand back there! You have held me up too long already!" he said roughly as he put the car into gear and sped away.

They next spoke to an old mule driver who was resting at the roadside. He looked kind, giving Lalu the courage to approach him and tell him what had happened.

The mule driver only gave them a long lecture about the dangers of dark, cool places where snakes often hide.

"One can go down into a baoli if there are several people all going together and making a noise. That would not be so dangerous. But to lie down in one and go to sleep is madness, for when everything is quiet the snakes come out. I should be very glad to help you, but I am a married man with eight children and I refuse to go near a cobra."

There was no one to help them. Despondently, they went back and sat for a long time at the opening without daring to go down. Finally Lalu ventured to go down a few steps while Kanga stood whining at the top.

The mat lay flat on the ground and no cobra was to be seen anywhere. Lalu grew braver and talked and shouted, pretending to be a great many people, and then went down the rest of the steps. Like lightning he swept together everything within reach, caught hold of a corner of one of the sleeping mats, shrieked wildly when a lizard ran across the wall, and then stumbled up to the two who were waiting for him above.

Maya wept: "Did you see it again? Did it strike?"

"No—I don't know what I saw."

The only thing he knew definitely was that he never wanted to go down into the baoli again. It hadn't brought them treasure; instead it had stolen one of their mats and most of their food. Silently Lalu and Maya tied their one mat around what remained of the dried fish, and continued their way along the highroad.

7

THE ELEPHANT

The days passed and Lalu and Maya plodded on. Patiently they trod the road, from dawn to midday, from afternoon to dark. Kanga followed them like a shadow. Their worst fear, the fear of the police, had ceased to trouble them since Jhandu had put the policeman onto the wrong track.

In a bazaar they bought a little saucepan, two wooden bowls and some food to take the place of the things they had left behind in the baoli. All this took a lot of the money Lalu had been carrying in his belt, but he realized it was necessary. Hungry as they were, they could hardly keep going without rice and ghee, and they couldn't afford to buy more expensive food. Kanga suffered, too, as there was not much food for a starving dog to be found along the hard dry road. What with the lack of food and the dust, she had become sadder-looking than ever.

They divided their food every day into three portions.

Kanga swallowed hers in one gulp, and then, with long-ing eyes, sat watching every bite the others took. Maya couldn't bear to see her sitting there envying every mouthful she ate, so she would turn around and sit with her back to the poor animal. But Kanga always followed after her, begging for just one more bite.

"Kanga, you have had just as much as I have! Why can't you eat slowly as I do, instead of swallowing it all in one mouthful?"

"Don't beg, Kanga," Lalu would add sternly.

Kanga's ears would droop and she would be quiet for a moment. Then she would begin to whine again.

One day they heard drums and flutes from far away, and came to a little village where it was a feast day with a procession to the temple. The temple lay on the bank of the river Jumna, which flowed along broad and calm, almost like the holy Ganges. The children in the village were putting small clay bowls on the water with lighted candles in them. If their bowls reached the far shore with the candles still alight, they thought their prayers would be answered.

Maya and Lalu joined the happy procession in which everyone carried flowers and fruit as an offering to the god in the temple, and they each were given a handful or two of the good food which was distributed in the temple yard to the poor and the sick. They hadn't felt so joyful since leaving home. Everybody was friendly and gave them bananas and smiled at them.

"What pretty eyes you have," they said to Maya.

"How pretty she is," they said to Lalu. "Here is another banana for you."

They had not been so well fed since the day they parted from Jhandu.

When the sun set over the broad river it made the water look like flowing gold. The small clay bowls with their burning candles bobbed up and down on the shining surface like stars in a golden sky. Maya longed to buy a candle and a bowl so that she could see whether it would sink or float, foretelling whether they would get to Agra or not. But of course they could not afford such things. She and Lalu had to be content with shouting and singing along the river bank with the other children, and watching the sunset change into red and then violet, coloring the gray huts in the village until they looked like small palaces.

At last they had to tear themselves away and prepare to leave. Then quite suddenly they saw a very strange sight.

On a height behind the temple stood a great, gray elephant decked out in festival array. It stood there unmoving against the flaming evening sky. Its head was painted in strong colors and decorated with red velvet and gold tassels, and around it scurried a crowd of children and older people.

"An elephant! Watch for a great, gray elephant!" the Guru had said. A thought rushed through Lalu's brain.

Was this animal going to bring them luck, and perhaps shorten the road to Agra?

He and Maya ran over and stood watching it with the other village folk.

The elephant's gold and red velvet coverings lent glamor to the festival, and so did a fourteen-year-old boy, dressed in white silken garments and a bejewelled turban, who was preparing to mount the canopied seat on the elephant's back.

"Who is he?" asked Maya as she pulled at Lalu's shirt-sleeve.

Lalu could not answer, but a man in the crowd said:

"It is the Maharajah's eldest son. His name is Nawab Khan."

The elephant knelt down and then it looked more like a mountain than ever with the canopy sitting like a little house on the top.

Involuntarily, Lalu went nearer and stood there hesitantly:

"Watch for a large gray elephant," the Guru had said. And here he was!

The crowd began to sing, and the wreaths of flowers the women wore smelled delicious. There was feasting and color all around the elephant and a drummer suddenly began to beat his drum with his bare hands.

At this moment, when the young Nawab Khan moved toward the elephant so that one of his servants might help him to mount it, Kanga chose to do her one and only trick. She began to walk on tiptoe. She felt as though she were back in the circus again, with the open space all around her, the large animal in front of her, and all the people laughing, singing and milling about.

No one noticed her performance, at least not at first; they were all too busy looking at the elephant and the young Maharajah. But the young Nawab Khan saw her, took his foot off the first step of the ladder and laughed.

"Who owns this dog?" he shouted, clapping his hands.

In India people are used to seeing trained animals, but

Kanga was unique. She looked just like a little human being as she seesawed along, her forepaws hanging and her head nodding. It was a sight that might well make a Maharajah laugh.

"Who owns the dog?" he shouted again, as he had received no answer to his first question.

Bursting with the pride of ownership, Lalu stepped forward and said:

"The dog is mine."

"Will you sell her?"

Lalu shook his head.

"I'll give you a whole rupee."

"Oh, oh! A rupee, a whole rupee, for a starving mongrel!" shouted the people who were watching.

But Lalu shook his head.

"*And* a ride on the elephant!"

Lalu hesitated. A ride on a royal elephant was not an everyday event.

"Don't sell Kanga," Maya begged him, pulling at his arm.

"Look how thin she is," said an old woman.

"Sell her and she'll get plenty to eat."

"Nonsense," said a man in the crowd. "Pull a fish out of water and it dies."

"If you leave the dog as she is, she'll starve to death in no time," said others.

Kanga went on dancing, her paws hanging, her head bobbing up and down.

"Six rupees," cried the Nawab Khan a little impa-

tiently, "and a ride on my elephant." He moved a little
to one side so that Lalu could come closer to him.

"Will you give her enough food?" asked Lalu.

"I'll feed her myself," laughed Nawab Khan.

"And never beat her? Remember she has never been
beaten yet."

"I'll never beat her, I promise you. I'll see that she's
happy."

"Don't sell Kanga," begged Maya.

"Is it your dog?" the Nawab Khan asked.

"She belongs to both of us," said Lalu.

"Then up you come, both of you."

Lalu carried Kanga under his arm, Maya followed
reluctantly and they all three went up the rope ladder
which lay against the elephant's flank.

Lalu was completely bewildered. Climbing with his
bare feet, he felt as if he were going up a warm hill, not
an animal's back. Everything seemed like a dream.

There was plenty of room under the canopy for them
all to sit down. Suddenly the elephant rose, first on his
hind legs and then on his front ones, and it felt as if the
earth were trembling beneath them. Lalu and Maya
clung tightly onto the seat but the young Maharajah
only laughed.

"What's the dog's name?" he asked.

"Kanga," said Lalu unwillingly, as if he were revealing
a secret.

"Come here, Kanga. Here's some chicken for you,"

said the Nawab as he fumbled in a provision basket. Kanga ate the chicken in one mouthful as was her usual custom. She did not behave any more politely in the presence of princes than on the highroad.

"If only Kamak and all the boys at home could see us now!" thought Lalu as he looked down on the children far below him.

The young Maharajah went on feeding Kanga from his provision basket, scratching her behind her ear, and speaking kindly to her. The two seemed to have become good friends. Kanga appeared very much at home in the company of princes.

Lalu looked on. It was wonderful to see Kanga enjoying plenty of food for once, but surely she didn't have to forget her old friends so quickly?

"Where are you going?" asked the Nawab Khan.

"To Agra," Lalu answered automatically. He was still dazed by everything that had happened.

"To Agra? Then we'll have to ride for at least two weeks," laughed the Nawab Khan. "Elephants walk no faster than people. You'll have to content yourself with going only a very small part of the way."

He leaned over and shouted to the servant who was sitting on the neck of the elephant.

"Take us to the temple by the banyan tree and stop there."

"Certainly, your Excellency," answered the servant.

Lalu still felt as if he were dreaming. Here he was,

riding a royal elephant, an elephant which would perhaps bring him luck. Or would it? He had a strange feeling inside him, as if something dreadful was about to happen.

The sunset flamed into a deep red color that played over the elephant's purple hangings, making him appear even more extraordinary. As he passed by, the people along the road bowed and shouted: "Salaam! Salaam!"

Lalu no longer thought about Kamak and the boys in the village. The gnawing feeling that something was wrong was spoiling the whole ride for him. He felt sick in the pit of his stomach, and tried to make himself believe it was because he had eaten too many bananas at the festival.

Kanga went on munching chicken bones.

"Watch for a gray elephant," the Guru had said. "It may bring you luck." He would get six rupees for Kanga, the exact sum they had been obliged to spend to replace the supplies they had lost in the baoli. Surely it was good luck to get so much money. And Kanga would enjoy having chicken bones every day. And the Maharajah's son looked so kind. And Maya would have more food without Kanga, much more food. Surely all this was good luck. But why, then, did he feel so worried and sick?

Maya seemed to have forgotten Kanga completely. She sat staring at the sparkling precious stones in Nawab Khan's turban. They gleamed and glittered so beautifully in the sunset. It was seldom that Maya's weak eyes had seen anything so lovely.

"Are you very rich?" she suddenly asked, as if the question had been burning her tongue for a long time.

The young Maharajah shrugged his shoulders.

"Rich? Don't you know that all the rulers of India have been dethroned?"

"Yes." Everyone had heard that the rulers had been dethroned when India had become self-governing, but Maya had never really believed it. Maharajahs and precious stones belonged to adventure, and Maya loved adventure.

"Look here," Nawab Khan said as he pulled at the ragged red velvet on the seats. "The stuffing in these seats is sticking out and the fringes are hanging loose. Our elephant stalls are empty. Nowadays most of the maharajahs live by selling their jewels in America and Europe."

"But you have not sold yours," said Maya, looking with admiration at Nawab Khan's glittering turban.

"No, we haven't had to sell these yet," said the boy, smiling in a carefree way. "And we still have a couple of cars."

They soon reached the temple. Nawab Khan took six rupees out of the purse in his belt and gave them to Lalu. The elephant knelt on the ground and Lalu and Maya stepped down the warm living hill of his back. Kanga clawed at the canopy and wanted to follow them but Nawab Khan held her back by the collar. She howled miserably. The young Maharajah's chicken bones might be tempting, but she wanted to stay with her friends.

"Be kind to her," Lalu shouted up to the Maharajah's son. "Goodbye, Kanga!"

"I will be kind to her, I promise you," shouted the rich young boy who was not really so very rich. "Kanga shall have a good life!"

He smiled with his pretty white teeth and the elephant swung into a side road on its way to the palace.

Then Lalu and Maya went on again toward Agra—but without Kanga.

8

THE SIGNALMAN

For the next few days nothing out of the ordinary happened. The weather was very warm for winter but the nights began to be chilly. One night they found a good sleeping space on the outskirts of a village and lay together on their one sleeping mat, sharing their single woolen blanket, and shivering until they got off to sleep.

In the middle of the night Lalu woke up feeling that something was close to him. He was wide awake in a moment. All was silent. But when he had lain quite still for a while, looking around him in all directions, he suddenly noticed a pair of glowing eyes in the darkness beyond the clearing. They frightened him and he took the saucepan and threw it with all his strength in the direction of the eyes. It fell jangling to the ground, and the eyes disappeared. Lalu lay for a long time wondering whether it was a dog or a jackal he had frightened away and shuddering at the thought of nights without Kanga to protect them. At last he fell asleep again and did not wake until the roosters in the village began to crow.

In the afternoon they came to a level crossing where they had to wait for a train that was late. A long row of cars, tongas, mules and cyclists stood patiently in line in front of the barrier. The beggars were very busy stretching their begging bowls up to the windows of the cars. It was very hot since there were no shade trees on this stretch of road.

Bird vendors carrying stacks of bird cages circulated through the crowd, offering their wares. Small performing monkeys did their tricks and their owners had a few coins thrown to them from time to time. A snake charmer came along with two baskets hanging at each end of a bar which he carried over his shoulders. He took out a pair of sleepy snakes and coiled them around his neck, but he did not open the basket containing the dangerous cobra. The train might come by at any moment, and then the cars would go off without paying anything for the show.

But the train did not come.

Lalu and Maya sat chewing dried fish to pass the time. They were hungry and tired and they had seen enough of performing animals to last them their whole journey.

"You should not have sold Kanga," said Maya.

"Shut up!" said Lalu.

"She might have done tricks like that monkey over there and we could have earned a few annas too."

"You know well enough that Kanga only did tricks when she felt like it!"

"You speak about Kanga as if she were dead. As long as she isn't dead . . ."

"Oh, be quiet."

"And the dried fish you bought is moldy."

"You're moldy yourself."

They sat with their backs to each other, quarreling. There was still no sign of the train.

A signalman in khaki uniform came out of his house and walked slowly along the rows of vehicles, inspecting them all. He looked into the cars and carts and then stopped a moment in front of the children. Looking hard at Lalu's thin body and Maya's shabby cloth bag, he asked whether they were alone or with a party.

"There's only us two," answered Lalu, wondering why he was looking so suspiciously at them. The signalman went away but came back after a moment and looked closely at them again. Then the train came by.

It was a very long and incredibly overcrowded train such as one sees only in India. People filled every available seat and were so tightly packed in the corridors that they could hardly get their hands up to their mouths. It took a long time for the train to pass.

When it was already far out on the plain, the barrier still had not been raised. The waiting cars began to honk their horns, and the impatient cyclists rang their bells.

At last the signalman climbed up on the gate and swung a red flag.

"Listen to me! Stop all that honking and jingling!" He waited for silence before going on:

"There is a thief among you," he shouted.

A chauffeur stuck his head out of his car.

"Raise the barrier! We can't stay here the whole afternoon just for the sake of a thief."

The signalman waved the red flag.

"Silence I say. The owners of the stolen goods have

promised a hundred rupees for the capture of the thief. That money I intend to earn, and I have full authority from the police to search anybody I think it advisable to search."

Again there was restlessness in the rows of cars before the barrier and the signalman blew his whistle and swung his flag.

"Silence. I have more to say. All cars may pass when I lift the boom. But those on foot must stay behind and allow themselves to be searched. There is a thief among them."

The boom was lifted, and all the cars, carts and bicycles moved forward and disappeared in a cloud of dust. The oncoming traffic from the opposite direction began to push its way over the rails through the crowd of beggars, monkeys and pedestrians.

The signalman stood, legs apart, in the middle of the rails.

"Cross here!" he shouted to the frightened beggars. "All adults may pass!"

The beggars shoved their way past the boom, and ran or hobbled along the road, terrified lest the powerful man should change his mind and stop them again. All children in the charge of adults were allowed to go.

But when Lalu and Maya approached the barrier, they were stopped.

The signalman fixed his gaze on Maya. "Green trousers, red blouse, blue eyes. You're the girl all right." He turned to Lalu. "You've pulled off your shirt, but I'm sure you're the boy. Come this way!"

Ever since the policeman from Allahabad had turned back to search the villages instead of continuing along the highroad, Lalu and Maya had felt secure, but now disaster had suddenly overtaken them at the peaceful railroad crossing.

All the travelers had passed now and they were left alone with the signalman. Grasping them roughly by the arm, he led them away to his cottage, a low house of gray clay with a roof of palm leaves.

He took them into the house, a single large empty room with a clock on the wall. A woman was sitting on the floor shredding rice into a bowl.

"Search the girl," said the signalman as he pushed Maya across the floor toward the woman. "She and this boy have stolen a diamond ring from the wife of the moneylender in Katwa."

Lalu stood there as if turned to stone. So this was the reason why the policeman and the signalman had chased them day after day as if they were criminals. Akvi had lost a diamond ring. He vaguely remembered seeing a red sari and some jewels on a stool, on that day, a long time ago, when he went with his father to the money-lender. He had scarcely looked at them; he had been too engrossed with the radio. Rage boiled up within him.

"It's not true," he shouted as soon as speech came back

to him. "We have not taken any ring, we have not taken anything at all. You just search us!"

"That is just what I am going to do, but you might as well confess now. The description tallies in every detail, age and everything. Why, the girl even has blue eyes."

"That is the only true thing you have said, but it is not enough to—. We have not taken anything, I tell you!"

"Be quiet, boy."

It was useless to say anything. Lalu had to stand and look on while the signalman's wife undressed and searched the crying Maya, shaking out her trousers and tunic, and even undoing her neatly-braided hair. But the only thing she found was the little bag full of tiny stones and pieces of broken pots.

"There is nothing here," she said, "unless there is something in this." She threw Maya's treasures over to the signalman.

The man shook them out and threw both them and the bag on the floor.

"Only rubbish!" he said. "Look after the children while I deal with the freight train that's due."

He cast a glance at the large timetable on the wall and went out.

"Dress yourself," said the woman to Maya.

"And you," she added, pointing to Lalu, "pick up all that rubbish on the floor. That will keep you out of mischief!"

Lalu picked up the bag and collected the blue and the green pieces of pottery and the small fragments of white marble. As he dropped in the last one, a thought rushed through his head. "My money! If the signalman sees money he will think I've sold the ring and kept the money."

Quick as lightning he removed the purse from his belt and pushed it down into the bag with Maya's treasures.

"You hold onto this," he said to Maya, shoving the bag quickly into her hand.

"All right," answered Maya obediently. She wondered why the bag had suddenly become so heavy, but she knew better than to say anything. The house shook as the freight train rumbled past.

At last the signalman came back and told Lalu to undress. He examined the boy, and every pocket, fold and seam of his clothes and his sleeping mat, but found nothing except a piece of Kanga's collar and a half-chewed stalk of sugar cane.

"Is the ring in your mouth?" he demanded. "Open."

Lalu was furious, but was forced to open his mouth and let the signalman stick his dirty fingers into it.

"Have you swallowed it? Answer!"

"I have never taken any ring!"

"Silence!" the signalman was angry. Apparently he wasn't going to get the one hundred rupee reward so easily after all.

"Well, we'll see. But the description fits perfectly. Two children, seven and thirteen years old, wandering like beggars along the highroad. And the girl has blue eyes. I'm going to put you both under arrest. If you don't hand the ring over by tomorrow morning early, I'll send you both back to Allahabad."

Without saying a word, Lalu bent down and collected his clothes. He felt completely defeated. Tomorrow morning they'd be taken back to Allahabad; they had walked all this long way in vain.

It was almost dark when the signalman took them both out to the stable where an ox stood tied up to a pole, chewing his cud, while a mule munched hay beneath a small square opening in the roof. Shoving Lalu and Maya inside, the signalman shut the door behind them and bolted it.

As soon as they were alone the children collapsed onto the floor. Maya was crying no longer. Instead she sat there banging her clenched fists on the floor.

"If I had Akvi here, I'd pull her hair till she screamed. I wouldn't touch her dirty rings. She's a witch."

Lalu lay down full length. Never in his life had he felt so tired.

"Was it your purse that made my bag so heavy?" Maya asked, bringing the bag out. "Yes, it was! Clever Lalu!"

"What good is it?" said Lalu in a tired voice. "The police in Allahabad will take it. Everyone is a thief except us."

"But the signalman didn't get it at any rate. Clever Lalu! You are much cleverer even than Nani."

Maya's open admiration did Lalu good. His eyes grew

accustomed to the darkness, and the calm chewing of the ox was almost restful. Before they knew it they were both fast asleep.

Later in the night they woke when a train thundered past. They heard the barrier go down and the furious voice of the signalman's wife talking to herself. Obviously it was she who looked after the crossing at night.

Lalu wept a little in the darkness. Everything was lost because of a ring which they had not taken. Neither he nor Maya could walk the long way from Allahabad again, he was sure of that. Maya would become blind, and neither of them would learn to read or write. All was indeed lost.

"Are you crying, Lalu?" Maya's voice came to him across the warm darkness. Lalu had thought that she was asleep.

"I'm not crying. My nose is just full of dust and hay," he lied.

"I'm so furious with Akvi!"

"It makes no difference what we feel."

At dawn, a pink tinge of daylight came down through the little square opening in the roof and made the stable lighter. Lalu woke to see Maya sitting on the floor, her face turned upwards.

"Do you see that hole up there, Lalu?"

"Yes, what about it?"

"Do you think I could squeeze through it? I'm much thinner than I was, you know."

Lalu got up. "It is too small and too high up."

"You could stand on the mule and hoist me up. I think I could manage to lift the latch on the door if I could only get out. It is exactly the same as the one we have at home."

"Let's try, Maya. We have nothing to lose."

Lalu stroked the mule who was asleep and chatted to it just as he used to chatter to Surmi. It showed no sign of wanting to cooperate but Lalu climbed onto its back anyway, and raised himself slowly until he stood upright. Then he hauled Maya up after him and lifted her up to the little opening. The mule did not move. It was an obstinate mule and had decided immediately that it would not budge. Sometimes obstinate mules can be of use.

"If I can only twist my shoulders through sideways, I'll manage it," said Maya, easing herself up toward the opening head first. "Hold onto me, Lalu! Don't let go!"

Lalu clutched Maya's small thin legs.

"If only she doesn't stick so that she gets neither in nor out," thought Lalu. "If the signalman or his horrible wife finds her like that, they'll be more angry than ever."

The mule stood as if fastened to the spot, determined not to carry these disturbers of the peace anywhere at all. Maya did not utter a word, not even a groan. She was like a little snail half in and half out of its shell.

"What if a train should come just now," thought Lalu, but he did not say it aloud.

The stable was dark again since the opening was blocked by Maya's struggling body. Lalu was in a cold sweat in spite of the warmth given off by the sleeping oxen. He kept imagining that he heard trains coming and his heart was beating very fast. Then suddenly he saw a strip of red sunrise beyond the opening. Maya was through.

"Hold me, Lalu."

Lalu gripped the mule's back with his bare feet.

"I am holding you," he panted.

"She will kill herself, she will kill herself! Or else she will break her bones," he thought, and held on to her until his arms ached.

"There's hay beneath me. Let go!" he heard her say from the roof.

But Lalu was so worried that he couldn't let go even though he wanted to.

"Can't you hear me? My arms are in hay. Let go, Lalu! Someone may come!"

At last Lalu did let go and the mule, who was as unstable as all mules, suddenly changed its tactics and kicked out backwards. Lalu landed on the floor.

Soon afterward he heard Maya fumbling with the bolt outside the door, and so eager was he to get out of his prison that he pressed his body against the door, jamming the bolt. Maya said a lot of things which he couldn't hear, but he could tell from the tone of her voice that she was furious. He pulled himself together and yanked the door inward. The bolt gave way and Lalu tumbled back. But a moment later both he and Maya were standing in the light of the red sunrise, staring at each other, and scarcely able to believe that they were free once more. Then they both laughed aloud.

"We are free. We are free!"

"A train may come," whispered Lalu. They rushed inside and collected their things, both of them determined that they would leave nothing behind as they had been forced to do in the baoli. While they scurried about, the ox mooed in a friendly way in the half darkness. Then, bent nearly double, they ran along the shadow of the stable, slipped across the railway line where the green signals blinked at them, and ran as if chased by evil spirits along the road to Agra.

They ran until it was daylight. Perspiration rolled off them and they trembled with fear. Now and again they turned around and looked back and when it became too light for safety, they hid themselves as best they could in a bamboo grove not far from the road.

They said their morning prayers, and kept watch. Not long afterward they saw the signalman cycle past them at a furious pace, ringing his bell in an ill-tempered manner at all who got in his way.

"We can't go any further today," said Lalu. "When he doesn't find us he will turn back, but he mustn't meet us."

"Must we stay here all day and all night, too?" asked

Maya.

Lalu shook his head. "We can't do that. There may be snakes here."

For an hour they sat in the green, striped shadow of the bamboo grove, keeping their eyes fixed on the road, and talking about Akvi who had branded them as thieves.

"What in the world will Father say when he hears the police are after us?" wondered Lalu. "We who are respectable farmers."

"She is a witch. And her husband is bad, bad. He takes the land away from people when they cannot pay. Nani says so."

Hidden in the brushwood they sat and talked, and after a time they saw the signalman returning home. He looked much hotter and more uncomfortable than they.

Maya laughed, threw her braids back over her shoulder and spread out her toes.

"Did you see how hot he was? If only I could have hidden myself and seen his face when he found that the stable was empty!"

"We can go now," said Lalu.

They walked for a long time. Maya sang softly to herself. She thought she had done a good job that morning—and so she had.

But Lalu was very thoughtful. The road stretched out in front of them without trees or shade, losing itself in the endless plain. "What if this road only takes us to prison and not to the hospital?" he thought. "What if we do get to Agra only to be caught by the police there? We still have money for railroad tickets and could ride almost all the way home in a day. Should we turn back?"

He saw the train far away on the horizon wending its way across the plain. He suddenly felt so tired that he stumbled in the dust. His skin burned beneath his shirt where the signalman's hard fists had gripped him, and although he and Maya had eaten while they sat among the undergrowth in the bamboo grove, he still felt the taste of the man's dirty fingers in his mouth. And that man had branded him a thief! A common criminal! Those words stuck in his mind and sent angry tears into his eyes. Would it not be better to turn back, go home, and ask for help?

"Did you see how sweaty he was?" sang Maya. For her all danger was over, now that they had been able to outwit the signalman.

"Oh, do stop singing! We must turn around and go home."

Maya opened her eyes and stared at her brother. "Turn around? And run straight into the arms of the signalman?"

"No, no, we must take the train."

"Take the train? Use up all our money? Go home without my eyes getting any better, without money, without Kanga, without . . ."

Suddenly Lalu shouted.

"Shut up, you idiot! I can't go on any more. The next man who arrests us will probably take our money and let us go to beg along the highroad. Isn't it better to save our lives than our eyes? Can't I get that into your head?"

"Yes," said Maya quietly, and knelt down beside him. When Lalu sat down like this in the middle of the heat and just gave up, her whole world collapsed. She stroked his arms clumsily. "Come, we'll take the train home."

"We must go to the nearest station," said Lalu darkly. He got up, lifted their bundle and began walking again. A little later he asked a boy who was driving a flock of goats in front of him how far it was to the nearest railway station. The boy told him that if they walked fairly quickly they would get there by sunset.

But before they got very far, something happened that made Lalu change his mind completely. As they crossed the road to get into the shadow of some trees on the opposite side, they heard a howl from behind them. A gray shadow flashed through the dust, and a starving dog jumped up on Lalu, licking his hands and face wherever she could get at them, and whining with joy. It was Kanga!

Yes, it really was Kanga! She had neither eaten nor danced nor walked on tiptoe all the time she had been in the Maharajah's palace, and had finally managed to wriggle free of her chain. Then she had run back and forth until she reached the road again and got onto

Lalu's scent. Now she was with them again, thinner, dirtier and happier than ever.

"Oh, Kanga," wept Maya, patting and stroking her. "You don't know how we've missed you! Darling, darling Kanga!"

"You smell of home even if you have been living in a palace," laughed Lalu. All his depression and feeling of defeat had disappeared. "You're a fine girl. How did you ever manage to get away from the Maharajah?"

He looked at Kanga as proudly as if she were a royal elephant and not just a little village dog who had nothing to boast about except that she could walk on tiptoe.

They passed the railway station, and Lalu bought three fat pancakes, one for each of them. Now they would indeed have a feast!

They found a quiet spot, cool and green, in the shade of a leafy tamarisk tree beside a pool filled with water buffaloes. The sunshine filtered down through the branches and was reflected in the pieces of colored glass which Maya began to arrange in patterns on the earth in front of her. Of course they might be arrested again, and the road to Agra was as long as ever, but it was so peaceful by the pool that they once more felt hopeful. Kanga was with them, they had enough to eat, and a gentle breeze was cooling them, which they were sure had been sent by Chaya, the goddess of shade and compassion.

Kanga was half asleep with her head between her

paws, but her ears were raised in alert to catch any sound of danger, large or small, which might come from the distant plain. Knowing that Kanga was on guard, Lalu and Maya soon relaxed, fell asleep and slept until dawn.

9

THE LITTLE WEAVERS

The next day, on the highroad, Lalu discovered that they were now more than half way to Agra. Once he knew this, he had an even greater incentive to keep going. He had long ago learned, from helping his father plant the long rice field at home, that the second half of any big job always seems to go faster than the first.

But one fine day he and Maya had a scare that was quite different from any they had experienced before. It happened like this:

One Sunday evening at dusk they came to a weaving factory where the workers were all small boys. The patterns in the shining brocades produced in the factory were so fine that only children's fingers could arrange the threads. Lalu and Maya had never seen such a weaving factory before, but they were not surprised that the boys were working away at the looms on a Sunday evening. In India there are many millions of Mohammedans who shut their factories and shops on Friday instead of Sunday. And naturally the boys worked in the evening when it was cool, and slept at midday when it was hot.

The factory lay in a garden full of white flowering bushes, and the light from the weaving room streamed out across the lawns through the open door. High walls surrounded the garden, keeping out jackals and other stray animals, and making it look secure and inviting. A flight of steps led up to a porch which was still warm from the sun and a fine place to sleep in. Lalu asked a guard if they could enter it, and received permission to stay there for the night.

They made up a fire and ate a little. No one disturbed them. It was almost as if they had the garden to themselves. The flowers on the bushes only bloomed at night, and as it grew darker, their petals opened and filled the air with a sweet scent.

With a sigh of relief, Maya stretched herself out on the sleeping mat and went swiftly to sleep.

Before joining her, Lalu went for a walk around the garden and finally stopped at the door of the factory. He looked in at the great lighted room where five looms were working all at the same time. Behind the little weavers stood big strong boys who maneuvered the wooden board which lifted the warp up and down. The little boys, industrious as ants, were threading the tiny gold and silver silk spools in and out, two for every weave. They were at most ten or eleven years old, and probably even younger. But Lalu had never seen anything so eager as their thin boyish backs bent over the looms, nor had he ever seen anything finer than the shining golden brocades which they were making.

One or two grown men walked back and forth between the looms, examining the boys' work and praising it or correcting it, but they did not scold or punish. Lalu guessed that they were either the fathers or the grandfathers of the little weavers. In India most trades pass from father to son.

"How strange that they don't seem to grow tired, or run out into the garden every now and then to play," thought Lalu.

Suddenly he realized that another boy was standing beside him in the doorway. He was a thin, dark boy with matted hair, a few years older than Lalu. He had only one eye. Kanga began to bark violently, and Lalu, who was angry that she should bark so at a harmless stranger, scolded her until she stopped.

"What is your name?" asked the strange boy.

"Lalu. And yours?"

"Ramdas."

They stood for a while looking into the lighted weaving room. Ramdas sighed.

"If only I were a weaver! Is your father a weaver?"

"No, he's a farmer," said Lalu.

"A farmer? That's fine, too. How wonderful it must be

to live in one place, instead of wandering always from town to town. I wish my father were a weaver or a farmer."

"What is he?" Lalu wanted to know.

"A bear leader," said the boy, "and I am going to be one, too. We go from fair to fair and shout ourselves hoarse so that people will come and look. Then we yank the bear's nose ring until he dances, and my father and I crawl around on all fours in the dirt to pick up the money people throw. Most of the time we don't even make enough to eat."

Lalu turned around, and in the half darkness he saw

a large bear tied to one of the bushes. He realized now why Kanga had barked.

"Father has gone to buy some bread," said Ramdas. "He can't get much, for the show didn't go very well today."

"What happened to your other eye?" asked Lalu hesitantly.

"The bear knocked it out when I was only five years old. Bears get tired and hot from walking the highroad in their heavy fur and then they're cross and dangerous. They hate hot weather. It's cold and snowy where they come from."

"Where do they come from?"

"The Himalayas."

One of the boys from the looms got up and came over to them.

No one called him back, or told him that he must stick to his job during working hours.

"Is it true that you earn two rupees a day just for sitting still and weaving?" asked the son of the bear leader.

"We earn as much as four for the most difficult patterns."

The little weaver only reached to the middle of Ramdas' chest, but he held his head high and looked neither small nor weak when he straightened his back.

"We send brocades from here all over India, and all over the world, too. Would you like to see what I make?"

He brought a piece of material and unrolled it in front of the two boys. They looked at it in silent awe for it was as though all the riches in the whole world had been woven into that one little piece of material. It shone with color and glittered with gold and silver. Just looking at it was an adventure. The brocade itself told an adventure story, for on it was a picture of gods and men hunting, fighting and feasting in a jungle filled with animals, flowers and many-colored birds.

"Can you read, too?" asked Lalu.

"No, but I don't mind. Being able to weave is enough for me," said the boy.

He gave them each a tiny bit of silk and a piece of sugar cane and went back to his loom.

Lalu followed the bear leader's son over to the large shaggy animal which lay stretched out panting in the cool grass.

"Take care. Do not go too close to it. It's savage on days when it has only had a little food."

A rank smell came from the bear, and it was easy to see how thin he was under his fur. Lalu had seen many bears like him before, always wandering along dusty roads, always with a ring through their noses.

"Poor creature," said Lalu, who was used to the sleek buffaloes at home who were always well looked after.

"Oh, I expect he was a bad man in his former life," said Ramdas, "and this is his punishment. Father always tells me that if I run away from him and take a job on my own I'll be punished and perhaps reborn as a bear in my next life. Do you want it to dance? It's easy. All I have to do is pull the ring in its nose."

"No, leave him in peace," said Lalu.

A little later the bear leader himself came back. He threw a piece of bread to the bear and another to his son and was in such a bad temper that Lalu left as soon as he could. He went back to the porch and lay down beside the sleeping Maya. Kanga was restless because she could still smell the bear, but Lalu, not wanting any trouble with the bear leader, scolded her and at last got her to lie down.

An hour later the little weavers went home and the door of the factory was shut. The moon rose and shone on the white flowering bushes and the tired sleeping wanderers. All was silent, except for the two animals who were both restless, the bear because he had not had enough to eat, and the dog because she was afraid of the bear.

When the first pale light of morning appeared over the wall, and the white flowers shut their petals against the sun, Lalu dreamed that he was dressed in gold and silk and hunting in the enchanted forest which the weaver boy had shown him. Red and green parrots flew away in alarm when his dogs barked and drove a large animal toward him so that he might shoot it. He could not make out what kind of animal it was, perhaps a wild boar, perhaps a bear. He took careful aim, but didn't fire, because the dogs stopped barking and began to howl.

It was Kanga howling. The bear had broken loose from the bush to which he had been tethered and he nosed his way to the food beside Maya. He paid no attention to Kanga who was straining at her leash, her neck hairs bristling, and barking until she frothed at the mouth. He just went on calmly eating the rice that Lalu had put aside for their breakfast.

Kanga's barking finally woke Maya, who shrieked when she turned over and found herself looking straight into the muzzle of the bear. His great shaggy head and hot breath terrified her, and without even thinking of Lalu, she stumbled down the steps of the porch and ran as fast as she could across the garden and out the gate onto the open plain.

In his dream, Lalu was ready at last to fire his gun when he heard Maya clattering down off the porch, and he woke from his deep sleep only to see the bear, still busily eating.

"So it was a bear," he mumbled, remembering his dream. But he held no gun as he had in the dream. He was alone face to face with the great animal.

Still half asleep, he remembered Ramdas' words: "When we pull the rope he quiets down."

Lalu fumbled for the rope, found it, and pulled it with all his might. Immediately the bear fell back on his back legs and began to wave his forepaws like a child asking for forgiveness. Then he began to dance.

The bear leader suddenly appeared, awakened by all the noise, and it was difficult to tell whether he was more angry with the bear for breaking loose, or with his son for tying the bear up carelessly. Since he didn't know whom to blame, he boxed Lalu's ears instead.

It was a very hard blow and Lalu cried out. Now that the danger was over, he was furious, even more furious than the bear leader.

"What right do you have to hit me? You act just like a monster! If you had any courage you'd set the bear and your son free. They'd both be better off!"

The bear leader looked angrily at Lalu, but he did not hit him again. Without a word he turned his back to him and went off, for if a boy dared to speak like that to a grown man, the bear leader knew he must belong to a very high caste. Maybe he was a weaver, or perhaps even a Brahmin.

"Let's be off," he shouted across the garden to Ramdas. "See that you pick up all our things. The bear has eaten that Brahmin boy's food."

It was only now that Lalu realized that Maya was missing. He had been so busy with the bear and the angry man that he had forgotten her. He untied Kanga and led her out of the garden after him.

Maya was nowhere to be seen. Lalu shouted her name as he walked through the garden gate and out onto the road leading to the plain. But there was no answer. A flock of goats bleated in front of him, raising a cloud of dust which cut off his view of the road ahead. The morning sun was bright and hot.

He let Kanga go.

"We must find her, do you hear that, Kanga? She can't have gone far. Hurry, Kanga, find Maya!"

Kanga ran restlessly in circles, trying to find Maya's scent in the dust of the road where so many travelers had crossed and recrossed. She soon found it in the short grass by the roadside, and ran forward with her nose in the grass so quickly that Lalu could scarcely keep up with her. After running a few hundred feet they found Maya lying on the ground beside a clump of cactus. She was crying.

"Maya," cried Lalu, squatting down beside her and lifting her head onto his lap, while Kanga ran around and around, licking her feet. "Have you hurt yourself, Maya?"

"I want to go home," she screamed. "I don't want to go to Agra and get well. I just want to go home."

"You will go home, Maya. But we're a lot closer now to Agra than we are to home. We must get your eyes well first."

"I don't want to get my eyes well. I don't want to stay on this awful road. I want to go home."

"The bear has gone far away, Maya."

"I don't want to sleep on a step, I want to sleep on a roof, the roof of a regular house."

Lalu lifted her up. If only he could have carried her home, home to Mother or Nani, and not just into one strange place after another where there was no real shelter, and no food! The bear had eaten all their food and Maya needed it now, along with rest and quiet.

She was wailing because she had stumbled into the cactus, and both her arms and legs were full of tiny cactus thorns. Lalu knew what this meant. Many a time his mother and Nani had sat over him, pulling out cactus thorns from his skin. They were so tiny that it took hours, but out they must come. Otherwise they would go deeper in and enter the bloodstream which would spread their poison through one's whole body.

Bewildered, he carried Maya back to the garden, knowing no other place to go. Ramdas and the bear were nowhere to be seen. He laid her on the steps and began to pull out the thorns as best he could, but his rough, thick fingers could not get a good hold on them and Maya cried in pain. Trying to get her to think of other things, he told her about the man in the well, and the honey that dripped. But no story was exciting enough to make her forget the painful thorns.

For a time they were all alone in the garden, but then the little weaver who had talked with Lalu the evening before entered through the gate.

"What's the matter?" he asked, for Maya was still crying.

"She has thorns in her skin and I can't get them out."

"Let me see," said the weaver boy.

He handled her burning red skin very carefully so that the thorns would go no further in, as he patiently plucked them out one by one with his small, experienced fingers.

"I'm going to buy some food," said Lalu, for he was very hungry. "I'll be back in a minute."

"You won't be back in a minute if it's food you're after," said the boy. "There are no shops around here. Just wait a moment. The others will soon be here, and then we'll see what we can do."

A little later all the boys arrived. They crowded around Lalu and Maya like little squirrels, eager to be of help if they could.

"That bear leader—he is a bad man if ever there was one," said the spokesman for the boys. "We were more afraid of him than of the bear. But now we'll go and get some food for you."

They soon came back with a great deal of food, not only rice, but also sweet potatoes, and freshly-baked pancakes with ghee and bananas. They handed it all to Maya. Some of them fed her, because her arms were not yet free of thorns, while others went on picking the thorns out of her skin. One or two admired the treasures in her bag and arranged the stones in a lovely pattern for her to see.

As the pain lessened, Maya began to smile and laugh once more. She and Lalu stayed with the weavers most of the day and spent the midday siesta with them. It was not until late afternoon that they took to the road again, and by that time Maya's arms and legs were well on their way to healing.

꙲

꙲

꙲

10

THE BOY WITH THE BICYCLE

Maya's eyes had grown worse. She stumbled more often than before, and no longer played with her treasures when they stopped to rest. One day they were looking at a flock of peacocks feeding on the grass in a field when several of the larger birds opened out their glittering tails in the sunlight. Lalu expected Maya to clap her hands as she always did when she saw beautiful colors, but she scarcely noticed the birds, and Lalu realized that her eyes were no longer strong enough to see them. Then he knew how important it was for them to reach their goal as soon as possible, and he decided to spend some of their precious money to take a bus the rest of the distance. Surely, he said to himself, he would be able to earn a rupee or two for the return journey once they found their uncle in Agra, even though he knew there were hundreds of boys in India clamoring for every available job.

They joined the line at the first bus stop they came to and waited. Maya had been walking more and more slowly every day, and it had become almost impossible to wake her in the gray morning light when they had to be starting off. Riding the bus, they could reach Agra that very day.

The heavy machine, larger than an elephant, arrived at last in a cloud of dust. The waiting passengers climbed in and Lalu was lucky enough to find a place for Maya. The seat was so high that her legs hung down, but she was *sitting* and that was the important thing. He himself went and stood behind the driver's seat so as to be able to watch the steering. Neither of them had ever ridden a bus before.

Before starting up, the driver stood for a while on the road, munching betel leaves and spitting out the juice. Then he came down the aisle to collect the fares from the new passengers, but when he saw Kanga he yelled:

"Who owns this horrible little dog?"

"I do," said Lalu, stepping forward. He felt like saying that Kanga was *not* a horrible little dog. But the driver looked so fierce that he did not dare take the chance of making him angrier.

"Out you get! Dogs are not allowed in the bus!"

Lalu stood absolutely dumb. Kanga couldn't be expected to run after the bus all the way to Agra. It was one thing to follow a slow-moving ox wagon with Maya's scarf dragging behind it, but quite another to run after a speeding bus for many hours with gasoline fumes blowing in her face.

"I will pay for her," said Lalu meekly.

"Didn't you hear me say that dogs are forbidden in the bus? Anyhow, we're crowded enough without dogs!"

"She can sit on my knee."

"Dogs have to travel in boxes, just as on a train."

Of course Lalu could not get hold of a box, so there was nothing to do but haul Maya down from her seat where she had settled herself so comfortably. The three of them soon stood on the dusty road again, watching the bus go off.

That afternoon they stopped to rest on the outskirts of a village, since Maya was walking more and more slowly. Lalu took Kanga with him and set off across a nearby pasture in search of buffalo dung for their fire. When he came back Maya was very upset. Ever since the trouble with the bear, she had been afraid of being left alone.

"What if the bear had come past? What if you had never found me again?" she wept.

"Don't talk nonsense," said Lalu. "The bear is tied up anyhow, and Kanga would soon pick up your scent even if I did lose you. Look how much fine dry fuel I have found."

"I thought you had lost me when you stayed away so long," wailed Maya.

She soon quieted down when Lalu expertly built a

fire between two stones and began cooking their main meal of rice. There was a full bowl for each of them. As they neared Agra, Lalu had been more and more generous with the size of their portions. Now he decided he'd better count their money again. They had only ten rupees and eight annas left, and he hid them away in his belt.

They found a good place to stop for the night in front of a thick hedge which shielded them from the night wind. Although it was still light, Maya sat with her eyes closed and her head bent as if she could not hold it up properly.

"Tell me the story of the boy who sat in the well until honey dripped into his mouth," she begged.

But Lalu said that he would save that story for the very first night they got home and were lying on their own roof again. Instead he told a story about Indra, who created the mountains of the world.

"In the beginning the mountains hovered in the sky on black wings like great huge birds," Lalu said, just as Nani had taught him. "Then one day Indra cut the wings off the largest mountain and set it down on earth. Afterwards, he planted the smaller mountains all over the world, wherever he thought they fitted in best. But their wings stayed up in the sky and were turned into thunder clouds. In bad weather they can be seen to this day."

"Did all the mountains used to float in the sky? The Himalayas too?"

"The Himalayas too," said Lalu. He sat caressing Kanga's ears, which were as soft as silk. Then, just for fun, he tied Maya's red scarf around Kanga's head and put a little bamboo stick between the toes of one of her forepaws. Kanga began to walk on tiptoe and dance and she looked so funny with the stick and the scarf that Maya laughed and laughed. She and Lalu were enjoying themselves so much that neither of them noticed a boy leaning against a bicycle on the road above who was looking on and laughing with them. Then he rang his bell, startling them both.

"Will you sell your puppy?" asked the boy.

"She is not for sale," said Lalu shortly.

"Then will you exchange your puppy for this bicycle?"

Lalu's eyes opened wide. He had never imagined that anyone would want to sell his bicycle if he were lucky enough to own one, not even for a dog that walked on tiptoe and danced.

"She is not for sale," repeated Lalu, looking at the bicycle.

It was a rusty, shaky old machine, he could see that with one eye, but it was a bicycle after all, no doubt about that. The tires were good and it had a carrier on the back.

With such a bicycle he could get to Agra in no time and use his money for food instead of railway tickets.

"Get up onto the carrier and I'll take you for a ride," said the owner of the bicycle. He was a heavily built boy of about fifteen.

"Don't do it, Lalu," begged Maya, "don't leave me!"

"Or ride the bicycle yourself and let me sit at the back," said the owner. "Or perhaps you can't ride."

In Lalu's village, bicycles were a glory that fell to the lot of very few, but the owner of the sugar mill had one, and he had allowed Lalu to borrow it now and then as a reward for minding the mill for a couple of hours. Lalu couldn't bear to have this boy think he didn't know how to ride one, so he jumped across the ditch and laid his hand on the handlebars.

"Don't leave me," said Maya weakly.

"I'm only going to take a turn down the road. I'll be back in a minute," said Lalu. "Here, hold Kanga's collar. She'll be company enough for you."

He swung himself up onto the bicycle in a practiced way, and waited a moment for the owner to get onto the carrier behind him before cycling off at a good pace down the road.

Behind him he heard Kanga barking and Maya shouting to him, as if they were both calling him back as loudly as they could. But Lalu paid no attention, for it wasn't every day that he was able to ride a bicycle.

"It has both a back brake and a front brake," boasted the boy behind him in his queer cracked voice. Lalu had to try both the back and front brakes. The miller's bicycle only had a front brake. It was fun to brake suddenly at full speed.

"Go faster," cried the boy. "The tires have just been pumped up."

Lalu increased his speed. He rang his bell and people moved quickly out of the way. He rang his bell louder and louder, and children ran in all directions. He had the power to make people move out of his way. The wind caressed his ears and cooled his chest and arms as he sped on toward the sunset.

What would his friends say if he came home with a bicycle of his own?

"What would your father say if you exchanged this bicycle?" He threw the remark back over his shoulder.

It was very unlikely that the exchange would go through, even if he made up his mind to accept it.

"He has sense enough to agree," said the voice behind him, suddenly cracking.

"Would he rather you have a dog than a bicycle?" asked Lalu suddenly. Dogs abound in all villages while bicycles are something that cost money. For a moment he wondered whether he should offer his ten rupees and eight annas for the bicycle, and ride straight to his grand-uncle in Agra. But he knew well enough that a bicycle like this was worth ten times more, no matter how much it had been used.

"Bicycles cost a lot to keep up," said the cracked voice. "But one can make money with trained animals. I stood looking at your dog for a long time."

Suddenly Lalu braked. He sprang off the bicycle. It was as if he had waked from a dream. Why, he had been on the point of selling Kanga for a second time, and not just as a plaything to a maharajah, but to someone who wanted to use her, beat her, starve her into obedience. He had seen enough of trained animals on his journey along the highroad.

"The dog is not for sale," he said shortly. "Come on, let's turn."

He and the boy stood looking at each other face to face. The boy realized that he must have said something that had spoiled the deal for him.

"Don't be stupid! I'll do nothing to the dog that you wouldn't do yourself. I'll just let it dance."

"Will you take ten rupees for the bicycle?"

"Ten rupees!" The boy burst into a roar of laughter. "I want your dog. Can't you hear me?"

"Come on! Let's turn," said Lalu. He had finished with his dream of owning this bicycle.

"Turn? Oh, no! You can walk back on your own two legs, my friend!"

Lalu turned his back on the boy and began to walk back the way he had come. He held his spine straight and his head high. A stream of bad words followed him as he went.

"You son of a mule! Your mother's shame! You should give me that money just to pay for the ride you've had!"

How many blows and kicks would such a scoundrel have given Kanga every day? And he had been near to selling her! Lalu walked quicker than ever until he could no longer hear the boy's insulting voice.

It was incredible how far he had traveled in so short a time. The village was nowhere to be seen and it was growing dark. The short dusk of the tropical night had set in, and to Maya who walked in half darkness even in the bright sun of day, it would seem pitch black. He began to run.

The jackals gathered in groups out on the plain and began to howl their evening song. Lalu knew only too well that they always grew bold in the darkness and sometimes even ventured right into the villages to steal a hen, eat an animal that was already dead, or attack small children if they could get at them. And Maya was sitting by the road, helpless and alone.

Lalu began to run like a madman. Maya and Kanga were alone with the jackals. He had betrayed them both for the sake of a ride on a bicycle. He could not even find the village, but he knew that it lay right beside the road so he was bound to find it sooner or later. He ran so fast that his chest began to hurt when he breathed.

Suddenly the first houses in the village came into view just ahead. He had heard the village before he saw it, children shrieking, mothers scolding, and the sound of lutes being played beside the evening fires. Lalu heaved a deep sigh of relief. But where was the place they had been resting in? It was somewhere on the outskirts, he knew, but where!

"Maya!" he called to the right and to the left, feeling suddenly quite bewildered. Was the place on this side of the village or on the farther side? Had he cycled through the village on his way out, or hadn't he? Why were the miserable jackals howling worse than ever? There must be hundreds of them!

No, he had not cycled through the village, he remembered that now. Then where were the bushes that had protected them from the wind? There! He was sure he'd found the spot and hunted all around it. But no one was there.

"Maya, Maya!" he shouted, feeling more certain than ever that the jackals had eaten her.

His cries echoed far out over the plain but there was no answer.

He stopped and looked around him in the dusk. This was the place, all right. There was no mistaking it. He ran on ahead a little, then back in his own tracks, looking for some trace of them, or a sign of the direction they'd taken.

"Maya!"

He had almost given up all hope when he suddenly bumped violently into Kanga, who jumped high up onto him with a long, sobbing whine.

"Oh, Kanga!" He knelt down, patted her, and hugged her close to him.

"Where have you hidden yourselves? I thought you were both dead!"

Kanga whined and panted as though she had just run across the whole plain. Her tongue was hanging far out of her throat.

Suddenly Lalu realized that his hand was covered with blood.

"But what's this, Kanga? Blood?" He bent down over her and now he saw that one of her ears had been chewed right off.

"Kanga, you've been fighting! You've been fighting with the jackals!"

He tore off his shirt and wrapped it tight around Kanga's head to stop the bleeding. Then a new terror struck him.

Maya! Where was Maya?

Kanga began to whine again, and insisted that Lalu put her back on the ground. Then, despite her pain, she began to limp off down the road. Lalu realized she was leading him to Maya!

He found her on a patch of grass farther down the road, fast asleep. Two women from the village were bending over her. He pushed them aside.

"Are you hurt, Maya? Did the jackals attack you?"

"She's asleep," said one of the women. "Though how she can sleep through all their howling, I don't know. She must be completely exhausted."

Lalu lifted Maya's head up from the earth, turned her over, saw that she was unhurt and threw himself down beside her. She must have cried herself to sleep for her face was wet with tears.

He pulled out a rag from his belt and dried all traces of dirt and tears from her sleeping face. She had had so little chance to rest lately that when she did fall asleep it was almost impossible to wake her.

"The day after tomorrow," said Lalu remorsefully, "the day after tomorrow, perhaps even tomorrow, we'll be in Agra."

"Where have you come from?" asked the same woman who had spoken before. "Are you pilgrims?"

"We're going to the hospital in Agra," said Lalu. "There's a doctor there who makes sick eyes well again."

"Come along home with me," said the woman. "It will

be better for you to stay with me tonight. It's not safe here. There are too many wild animals out on the plain, and the jackals are dangerous, too, especially to helpless children." She lifted the sleeping Maya up and carried her off.

"My name is Asha. What is your name?" she asked.

"Lalu. The son of Kumar Nagh in the village of Katwa east of Allahabad."

"Allahabad!" gasped Asha. "Have you come all this way alone? For you are alone, aren't you?"

"We have walked," said Lalu.

"Walked? No wonder this little one here is worn out. She weighs nothing at all."

A crowd of children surrounded them when they entered the village and plied Asha with one question after another.

"What is the matter with her? What has happened to the dog? Has she been fighting with jackals?"

"The dog has saved this child," said Asha. "Get out of the way so that I can get into my house with her."

She took a sleeping mat down from the wall and spread a blanket over the sleeping girl. Maya murmured a little, then turned over on her side and went on sleeping.

Lalu sat with his back against the wall of the house and took Kanga into his arms. She had suddenly become the heroine of the whole village, and voices hummed all around her.

"The little mongrel has saved a child from the jackals. Have you heard about it? Those horrible jackals."

Someone brought water which Kanga drank greedily. Others brought Lalu's and Maya's possessions, their sleeping mats, saucepan and food. Nothing was missing. Someone else fetched the village veterinarian who bound up Kanga's ear securely and put a collar on her so that she would not scratch at the wound.

"Such a thin little mongrel cannot stand losing much blood," said the vet, fastening the bandage carefully. "See that she does not pull or tear at it."

But Kanga did not feel like pulling or tearing at anything. She crept close to Lalu and seemed terribly upset at being the center of so much talk and to-do. Lalu sat with her the whole night after everyone from the village had left, and the rest of the household had gone to bed. She was shivering a little with fever, and sometimes whined in pain, but when Lalu stroked her she quieted down.

They stayed with Asha for two whole days. Maya played with the village children who thought she was wonderful because she had almost been eaten by jackals. She wanted to stay there always, but Lalu knew that Asha had enough to do with her own children. Besides, Maya's eyes were getting worse every day. They had to leave. They thanked Asha politely for the help and hospitality she had given them. When she let them know how worried she was about their going on alone, they comforted her by saying that it was not far to Agra now, and besides they had friends and relatives there.

The village children followed them a long way when

they set out again on the highroad, but finally the last of them turned back, and Lalu and Maya were left alone again. In front of them ran Kanga with her bandaged head.

‎ʊ̈

‎ʊ̈

‎ʊ̈

11

THE SOCIETY FOR COMBATING BLINDNESS

The first night after leaving the village they slept in an inn with other travelers. Their experiences with the bear and the jackals had convinced Lalu that it wasn't safe to spend any more nights out of doors, even if it did save them money.

The sleeping room, in which everyone lay in rows on the floor, was so crowded and stuffy that Lalu and Maya decided to unroll their sleeping mats under a half roof that covered a veranda outside. Large bats hung by their feet along the end of the roof like black sacks, and as soon as it grew dark they let go of the roof one after the other and flitted noiselessly away to hunt for insects. Lizards ran across the floor and the walls, and all sorts of flying beetles and moths fluttered through the air toward the light in the sleeping room. Outside the plain stretched endlessly beneath the stars.

Lalu lay on his back under the half roof and made plans for the future. It was good to be able to relax in safety here and look at the stars, instead of feeling he had to be on guard all night. He felt strong and full of courage. He decided that the moment he got to Agra he would find the shortest way to his granduncle and ask him to help get Maya into the hospital. Once she had been admitted, he would look for a job. He didn't care what kind of job so long as he could earn enough money for their journey home.

They couldn't afford many nights like this one when there was a charge both for lodging and for cooking their rice on the stove. He must find some way for them to move faster than they had up till now. For although Asha had given Maya a pair of sandals for her sore feet, and he himself had slept soundly under a roof for three whole nights, he knew that they couldn't increase their walking speed enough to make any difference. Maybe he could beg a place for them on one of the carts here in the yard. Riding on it, they could reach Agra later in the day.

"Kanga can easily manage to follow a cart," thought Lalu as he fell asleep.

Next morning the two of them sat on the steps outside the inn, eating their rice and watching the other travelers carry out their luggage and pile it on bicycles and carts. Many of the carts were filled with children as well as luggage and went off overloaded with only one thin horse pulling between the shafts. Lalu could see that there was no room for him and Maya on any of them.

A man suddenly came out of the inn and went over to a bicycle which was leaning up against the wall. He was the tallest and thinnest man Lalu had ever seen, a whole head taller than ony of the others at the inn. While he was pumping up the tires, Lalu took his courage in both hands and approached him.

"Are you going to Agra?" The man nodded and went on pumping.

"When will you get to Agra?"

"At midday if the tires hold."

"Could you—could you take this little girl on your carrier and let her off in the railway station? I will give you a rupee."

"Two rupees," replied the man.

They bargained for a time and at last settled on a price of one rupee and eight annas.

Lalu folded the sleeping mat and put it on the luggage carrier so that Maya could sit on something soft. He gave her a couple of bananas to eat on the way, and told her to wait for him outside the station in Agra. Maya gave him no arguments. She was so tired of walking and so glad to have a chance to ride that for once she didn't even mind being parted from Lalu.

"You'll get the money from me," said Lalu to the man. "Wait for me at the station until I arrive."

"I want the money now," said the man.

"No. Not until I know Maya has arrived safely," said Lalu.

"But how do I know you even have any money? You don't look as though you do. Maybe you're trying to cheat me."

"If I wanted to cheat you I wouldn't have taken the trouble to bargain first. And you have a hostage in my sister."

To back his argument, Lalu fished out his purse and showed the man all his rupees, even though Jhandu had warned him not to show his money to anyone on the highroad.

"How many rupees have you got in there?" asked the man.

"Twenty," lied Lalu, pretending to be a rich man.

The man offered no more objections. Lalu helped Maya up onto the bicycle and stood looking after it as it swung onto the road behind the horse-drawn carts. Maya turned around and waved.

"Come as quickly as you can, Lalu!"

"I will come, Maya, never fear."

It was fine to be able to walk as swiftly as he liked, and not have to bother with Maya. He had often become impatient when he had to hold her hand, tell her stories to make her forget how tired she was, and stop for her to rest every half hour or so. Now he felt strong and free and broke into a run with Kanga at his heels. Traveling the highroad had strengthened him rather than wearing him down as it had Maya. He only realized this now.

The long-legged cyclist had not seemed to be pedaling very fast, and Lalu thought he could almost keep up with him on foot if he didn't stop or slow down. He had a fever in his blood now that the end of the journey was so near. He scarcely allowed himself time to eat, and keeping in the shadow of the trees, half ran all the rest of the way.

At last Agra appeared like a distant shadow along the horizon. *Agra!* Lalu had said the name so many times that his heart began to beat violently when it suddenly changed from a far distant goal to an actual city which he could see.

"Look, Kanga! Agra! Now things should be all right again, Kanga. No more highroads, no more jackals!" Kanga wagged her tail and stood on her head in an attempt to shake off her bandages.

Later in the afternoon, when the shadows became long, the indistinct line of buildings on the horizon changed into sharply defined roofs and temples. Lalu was very tired but he still did not slow down. If he could only keep going he would arrive in the city before darkness fell. He was very proud of the pace he had maintained. If Maya had been with him, it would have taken them two days to walk so far, if not three.

"How clever it was to persuade that long-legged cyclist to take her without payment in advance," thought Lalu, "and how clever to think of the railway station as a meeting place!"

Suddenly Maya ran out into the road directly in front of him, and squinted at him with her weak eyes as though trying to make sure it was really he.

Lalu could scarcely believe his eyes.

"Maya! What are you doing here? Where is the man? Where is the bicycle?"

"There!" Maya pointed under a big banyan tree whose air roots made a protective roof that reached right down to the ground. Sure enough—there lay the man asleep under it with his long legs stretched out.

"He has been sleeping for a long time," said Maya. "But I stood here in the sun because I was afraid of missing you. I can't see anything down there in the shadow."

Lalu was angry that the man had stopped so long. At the same time he was a little proud of himself for having caught up with him.

"He says that there is no room in the hospital," said Maya sadly. "That crowds of people have to go away without getting any help."

"Kamak's uncle was let in."

"He says that there is a society in Agra which is called" —Maya had to think for a moment—"The Society for Combating Blindness."

The long-legged one had now waked and was sitting up.

"It is no good, little one," he shouted, having heard what Maya had said. "Such fine societies are only for people who belong to a very high caste. They are not for just anyone."

"Do you call this driving straight to Agra?" asked Lalu angrily, pointing to the bicycle.

"Come down here and share the shade with me," said the man. "You've walked so fast you're sweating all over. If you want to know, I was afraid to go on. My back wheel has become so shaky that I think it will soon fall off."

They sat in the shadow of the banyan tree and drank water which the man gave them out of a goatskin sack. Lalu grew more amiable.

"Allow yourself to rest," said the man pouring out some more water. "It won't make any difference if you arrive one hour sooner or later."

A flock of monkeys jumped about and shrieked in the tree, amusing themselves by throwing branches and twigs down onto the three sitting below them. But in spite of them it was fine to be sitting in the shade drinking water.

"Ask him about that society," begged Maya.

"Well, I don't know much about it myself," said the man. "It is a society that fights all sorts of eye diseases in India. All I know is that it has helped many people."

"Do you think it could help us?" Maya wondered.

"It is not for everybody," said the man.

Lalu stood up.

"I thought you said that it fought eye diseases in India. Then it must be for everybody."

"What do I know? But tonight I am going to meet a man in an inn outside the walls of the town. He knows the Chairman. Ask him."

"All right," said Lalu. "We'll go with you to meet him."

He put Maya up again on the luggage carrier above the shaky wheel, and together he and the long-legged man wheeled the bicycle to the inn outside the city wall.

Many people were coming and going in the room where food and drink were served. The tall man had to bend his head as he stepped inside through the low door.

"Stay here until I come for you," he said over his shoulder. "I'll see if my friend is here yet."

Through the lighted window they saw that the room was full of people, but it was not difficult to keep an eye on the long-legged man. He was so tall that he towered above all the others. They watched him as he pushed his way through the crowd and joined a fat man in a turban. It looked as if he were trying to persuade the man of something, since he gestured a great deal with his hands as he talked to him.

Lalu hoped with all his heart that the man would agree to take Maya to the Society for Combating Blindness. It must be a large and powerful group. Perhaps it was the Society that had helped to get Kamak's uncle into the hospital.

Maya stood beside him, drooping with fatigue.

"Can't I lie down beside the bicycle," she begged. "There's enough room for a sleeping mat there."

"No, you wait! They'll soon come out to us and then we'll take the mat in. You must eat first."

At last the two came out and led them inside to a long table where they ordered supper. Lalu did not want to appear to be a poor boy, so he ordered rice soup for two even though it was quite expensive.

"My friend says that the Society is only for members," said the long-legged one. "The best doctors in the country belong to it and they have healed maharajahs and many grand people. I was right, you see. It is not for just anybody."

"How much does it cost to become a member?" Lalu wanted to know as he unpacked his and Maya's modest supper of sweet potatoes and a piece of milk cheese.

"I'm not sure, but I know it's at least ten rupees," said the man in the turban.

"I have only eight," said Lalu, "but I can earn the rest in Agra."

The man shook his head.

"Too little."

"Now, do be reasonable," said the long-legged man. "It may be that they would agree to take eight rupees for a child, especially if they're paid cash."

"Does the boy have the money with him?"

To prove he did, Lalu counted out his eight rupees onto the table and handed them over to the man in the turban.

"I want a receipt."

"Receipt? You want a receipt?" The man suddenly became very angry.

"All right, all right, since he doesn't trust us here's a pledge," said the long-legged man, and put a ring with a red stone into Lalu's hand. "We'll be back in a minute. You wait here."

With a little pang of regret, Lalu watched the two men go outside with the money. He saw the fat one sit heavily on the back of the bicycle on top of the wobbling wheel which suddenly seemed to be in good order again. Then they both disappeared from view. Maya put her head on the table and went fast asleep. These last few days she seemed to be sleepy all the time. Lalu himself sat up straight and looked out the window at the darkening sky where the stars were coming out. Every time the door opened he jumped up, and every time his hopes were turned into bitter disappointment.

Could people really be so cunning, accepting his last rupees as if they were doing him a favor, making him push the money into their hands and almost beg them to take it?

He delved into his memory to try and remember all that had been said, all the objections that had been raised to his and Maya's belonging to this society. He began to wonder if the Society even existed. Had they really deceived him?

The host, a big fat man who had been talking and laughing with the guests the whole evening, now came over to Lalu and told him that he must wake up the little girl and go. They were going to close.

Lalu answered that he was waiting for a message from the Society for Combating Blindness.

The landlord had never heard of such a society, nor did he know who the two men were who had eaten their supper there in his inn.

Lalu felt a great weariness come over him. He was too ashamed at having allowed himself to be taken in to accept it yet as a fact.

"Surely they can't just be thieves," he said. "Look, they gave me this as a pledge."

He handed the ring to the host who examined it.

"Rubbish from the bazaars," he said. "Glass and brass not worth more than a few annas."

Lalu sank down onto his stool.

"How much money did you give him?"

"All I had. Eight rupees."

The host banged the table with his clenched fist.

"The scoundrels! I'll go and fetch the police."

Lalu started as if he had been stung by a wasp.

"No, no! Not the police! Then *we'll* be arrested, not the thieves!"

"Nonsense," said the host. "You just stay here until I get back. It will only take five minutes."

"Five minutes, five minutes," mumbled Lalu to himself when the door banged behind the landlord. "Listen, Maya, we must get away."

The police again! And this time he actually *had* a ring. He shook Maya to wake her up but it was no good. He had to lift and drag her across the floor and out of the inn.

"Leave me in peace," she mumbled. "Can't you leave me in peace? You said I could sleep."

And she lay right down on the threshold. Lalu shook her again.

"Can't you hear what I say, the police are coming! Can't you understand? The police! The signalman perhaps . . ."

Maya only made herself more comfortable and rested her head on her arms. Lalu was about to pull her further away from the inn when he remembered his saucepan and sleeping mat, the only things he now owned in the whole world. He had left them behind in the inn. He scurried back inside for them, and when he came out again he ran straight into the arms of the police and the host who stood bending over the sleeping Maya on the threshold.

"Why is she lying here?" asked the innkeeper.

Lalu couldn't give any reasonable explanation for it, and after all, what did it matter? Suddenly he became absolutely indifferent to everything. His money had been taken from him in the most shameful manner, and he himself would be arrested instead of the thieves. Nothing could be worse than it was already.

"I haven't taken any ring," he burst out, "neither from the moneylender or anyone else! This ring is only bazaar rubbish." He stopped and leaned against the doorpost. For the first time on this difficult journey he gave in and began to sob.

"It is other people who take things from me and then blame me, who offer rewards of one hundred rupees, and hunt me as if I were thief and a beggar day after day!"

"Is your name Lalu?" asked the policeman, "the son of Kumar Nagh in the village of Katwa?"

"Yes," sobbed Lalu, "but I never took a ring. I have never stolen anything."

He was now crying so bitterly that he could scarcely speak.

"Stop your crying," said the policeman. "No reward is offered any longer for the capture of Lalu Kumar Nagh. It would have been so easy for me to collect it, too, since you walked straight into my arms. But the accuser has withdrawn the accusation. The ring has been found."

Lalu stopped crying.

"Has she . . . ?"

"Found the ring? Yes, in her own house. So I won't have a single rupee to thank you for."

Anger boiled up in Lalu. That stupid Akvi had not even troubled to look for the ring, so certain had she been that he was the thief because he was barefooted and poor and was going to Agra. Why, that horrible ring of hers might have landed him in prison, stopped the journey to Agra, and brought terrible punishments down on him when he finally got home. But now it had suddenly been found.

The policeman, a perspiring little man in a crumpled blue uniform, laughed at Lalu's confusion.

"You are lucky," he said.

"Yes, I expect I am," said Lalu weakly.

He gave the policeman an exact description of the two men who had gone off with his money but the policeman thought there was little point in looking for them since they had undoubtedly disappeared long ago in the crowded city. And anyhow there was no reward offered for finding them.

The innkeeper carried the sleeping Maya into the inn and let her lie on the bench. Lalu and Kanga lay down on the floor.

Next morning they were given a good breakfast and later in the day they walked into the town of Agra with full stomachs, but an empty purse.

12

THE ECHO

So here they were in Agra at last.

It was a smaller town than Allahabad, and much quieter. There were not so many people and no noisy market. Instead there were large green gardens filled with roses and Bougainvillaea surrounding hotels where Europeans with pale faces sat in deck chairs buying embroidery and snake skins from Indian merchants. Flocks of beggars waited for tourists outside the hotels, and so did hordes of small two-wheeled cabs pulled by men instead of horses.

Lalu and Maya looked into the shady gardens and wished they could lie down under the trees and watch the many snake charmers who sat on their heels playing the flute to their dancing cobras. They went on further and came to the market place which was literally bulging with food. A few days before, such a display would have made them very envious. But now, with the innkeeper's good breakfast under their belts, and the promise of finding their granduncle soon, they enjoyed strolling through the market and admiring the beautiful fruits and vegetables that were being sold.

They asked one or two people in the market if they knew Kadri Ali Singh, a servant to the rich merchant Ali Raza, but they only shook their heads.

At last they found somebody who showed them the way to Ali Raza's house. It was large and white with roses growing around it, and lay deep in a garden just like the fine hotels. It was so white and fine-looking that Lalu began to wonder whether he and Maya were not a little too dirty and travel-stained even to approach it, let alone knock on the door. He stood uncertainly gazing at the veranda while Maya tugged at his sleeve, impatient to be inside. At last he told her he thought they'd better clean themselves up before going any closer. She protested, but he led her behind the garden wall where they spent an hour trying to tidy themselves. Asha had washed their clothes and given Maya sandals before they left her house, but the dust of the highroad piles up just as thick on clean clothes as it does on dirty ones, making them all look equally gray.

Lalu told Maya to loosen her braids and shake out her hair until it shone, and then plait it neatly again in long, firm braids. While she did this, he gave Kanga's dusty coat a good brushing.

Maya kept on protesting. She was longing to see her uncle and thought Lalu was being unnecessarily fussy.

But at last he was satisfied. They left their belongings under a tree, and with straight backs, and a dignified air, walked up the long drive where the many tire tracks showed that this house had very few visitors who came on foot.

The drive swung into a large open area where tall bay trees had been set in pots, and stood as straight as soldiers at attention along the wall of the house. All doors leading into the house were wide open, and beneath the white pillars on the veranda a little girl guarded by an ayah was playing with her dolls.

Lalu and Maya approached slowly, followed by Kanga. The ayah, a dark skinned Hindu in a red sari, came down the veranda toward them. She seemed very surprised, as if it were the first time in her life that she had seen people walking instead of driving. Lalu and Maya put their fingertips together, touched their foreheads lightly and bowed.

"There is no admittance here for beggars," said the ayah without returning their salute, "and certainly not for dogs."

"We are not beggars, Memsahib," said Lalu. "We seek our granduncle, Kadri Ali Singh. Please fetch him."

The ayah looked still more surprised.

"Who is Kadri Ali Singh?" she asked.

"Our granduncle," repeated Lalu patiently. "He works for Ali Raza."

The little girl with the doll had come up and was holding on to the ayah and gazing at Lalu and Maya from behind her nurse. Now she laughed aloud.

"Ali Raza doesn't live here any more. He has sold the house to my father. We live here now."

Lalu suddenly felt quite dizzy. The pillars and bay trees began to sway in front of his eyes. "He doesn't live here? Where does he live then?"

"He has moved to Delhi."

Lalu did not know a great deal about the great cities of his country, but he knew that Delhi, where Mr. Nehru and the Government lived, was very, very far away.

"They moved almost a year ago," said the ayah who had not for a single moment ceased to look surprised. "But there's a train that goes there."

"I know," said Lalu in a low voice.

"I just finished combing my hair for the second time today so as to look nice for Uncle Kadri," said Maya, "and now he's not even here."

She and Lalu turned around and walked slowly away, their backs just as straight and dignified as when they came. They heard the little girl laughing behind them.

"Just imagine! They didn't know that we lived here!" she shrieked.

"Yes, that's really strange," said the ayah, still looking surprised.

The only thing Lalu and Maya could do now was find the hospital by themselves.

They asked the way, and at last stood in the street

before the enormous hospital buildings with their rows and rows of windows, more than they could count. The hospital in Agra is not one of the biggest in India, but to Lalu and Maya, accustomed to tiny village houses, it looked as big as a mountain range. They felt as if they had shrunk into small ants in front of such a mass of stone.

Honking cars made them scurry back and forth, and many people came and went through the hospital's huge entrance arch, streaming past them without looking at them, and sometimes shoving them when they got in the way. They were used to being pushed about in crowds, but all the same there was something especially depressing about finally reaching their long-sought goal, only to meet the same rude treatment they had suffered on the road. Lalu's courage failed him. He had no feeling of victory, and even felt reluctant to enter the hospital, whose buildings and people seemed so cold and uncaring.

For Maya, seeing everything through weak eyes, the whole scene lay shrouded in a sort of mist, and she was not nearly so depressed as Lalu. Blinking, she looked eagerly at the young students in white coats, both boys and girls, who walked past her, talking and laughing.

"That's what I want to be," she said. "When I have learned to read."

Lalu pulled himself together. They could not just go on standing here like this. They must go inside, get Maya treated and finish what they had started to do so long ago. He lifted the bundle with his saucepan and sleeping mat up onto his head, took Maya's hand, and together they tramped in under the shadow of the high archway.

But they had not reckoned with the guard. He suddenly appeared in front of them as if he had risen from the ground, a fierce-looking Sikh with a high turban on his head and a long beard parted in the middle. He stared at them belligerently, first at one and then at the other.

"Halt! What are you doing here?"

Lalu stopped and greeted him in the manner that was fitting when one met such a high-standing person.

"We . . . I . . . She is to be operated on, Sahib."

"Who has said so?"

"No one," said Lalu, confused. He could think of no words with which to impress the Sikh, who guarded the arch as if it were a holy place.

An ambulance hooted its way through, forcing them to the side. The Sikh saluted, raising his hand to his turban.

"There is no admission here except for those on business," he said, once the ambulance had passed.

If Lalu had only been able to read, he would have seen that there were fixed clinic hours in the hospital, and that he could have come back at one of those times, walked right past the dangerous guard, and entered without any trouble. But of course Lalu could not read. He thought that entrance was forbidden now and forever.

"Don't try to worm your way in by telling me stories," said the guard, who was about to lose his patience with Lalu and Maya. "Those who are to have an operation always come in an ambulance. Away you go!"

"We have walked the whole way from Allahabad," Lalu tried again, for he knew that their long walk made an impression on some people. But the guard thought that this was just another tall story. It was his job to keep away persons who had no real business in the hospital, and he meant to earn his pay.

"Oh, indeed! If you are strong enough to walk all the way from Allahabad, then you are strong enough to walk back again. Off you go!"

They began to wander about the streets without any objective in view. Maya started to whimper:

"Agra is a horrible town. There's no one here but stupid ayahs and stupid guards. What shall we do, Lalu?" But Lalu had nothing at all to suggest.

They stood for a time watching a building that was being built. A crowd of workers were cementing the stones, which their wives and children carried to them on their heads.

"If only I could get a job here!" thought Lalu. "Just earn enough to keep us from starving." He was stronger than many of these mothers and children who were carrying stones.

Carefully he approached a foreman, but only got sharp orders to get away.

"Wait until dinner time to ask for work! Off you go!"

They seemed to be in the way wherever they went.

Then Lalu suddenly saw a face he knew. He was so used to seeing only strange faces that he gave a loud and excited shout of surprise.

"Ramdas!"

It was true. There stood the bear leader's son looking at them with his one eye.

"Ramdas! What luck to meet you again! But where is the bear?"

"Dead," said Ramdas.

"Dead?"

"He collapsed the other day. I suppose he was tired of dragging along the highroad. We had to leave him to the vultures."

"Poor creature," said Lalu, but at the same time he felt relieved to know that the poor bear would suffer no longer.

"If one has a bad time in this life one gets on better in the next," said Ramdas. "It's much worse for my father and me. Now we've got no way of earning our living."

"What have you been living on?"

"We've just about starved, but now my father has landed a job at this building place. He only got it because I was along to carry all the building stones to him. That way, you see, they get the two of us for one man's wages. We are saving up to buy a well-trained monkey. Then we'll move on again."

"Do you think I could get a job on this building? We must get money for food. Maya could help me, so there would be two of us."

Ramdas took a look at Maya's fragile, narrow-shouldered body.

"She can't carry stones. Even with one eye I can see that."

Maya tossed her braids back over her shoulder and straightened her back.

"I have *walked* all the way from Allahabad."

"Yes, yes, of course. Well, you can always try. That's all anyone can do, I guess. Just try over and over and over again. But you said that she was going to the hospital."

"They won't let her in."

"No, they wouldn't let me in, either, when I hurt my eye," said Ramdas calmly, accustomed as he was to nothing but misfortune in life. "But it got better after a while. If you don't get a job, go over to that temple across the way and stand in line. They give out food to poor people once a day."

Just at that moment, Ramdas' father came over to them, storming with rage.

"You lazy boy, you! Here you stand jabbering while I'm waiting for stones. Perhaps you don't mind if we don't get any food today!"

Lalu took hold of Maya's arm and pulled her away from the angry man, and in a very short time both father and son were lost to view in the crowd of sweating, running and shouting workers.

Lalu did not get a job on the building. He lined up with all the others who were asking for work and tried to look as tough and grown-up as he could. But there were too many others who were tougher and more grown-up than he was. Then he and Maya went to the temple that Ramdas had pointed out, and stood in the line of poor people waiting for food. Here at last they had some luck and were given a portion of rice on a banana leaf.

After that they found a good resting place in the shadow of a wall. The thin sound of the temple bells filled the air and reminded them of Nani's peaceful morning worship in front of the holy image at home. Maya stretched herself out on the sleeping mat. Lalu sat with closed eyes. They began to feel homesick. Just at this time the buffaloes would be coming back from the field, eager and clumsy, pushing their way in through the doorway like hungry children asking for their supper. The children's small brothers would be pulling hay out of the stack for them. Their mother would be looking after the youngest child, and Nani would have a newly-baked pancake ready for them. Home—the only place in the world where they were always welcome, however little room there might be in the house.

When Maya went to sleep, Lalu tied Kanga to a ring in the wall and told her to keep guard. Then he went off to the building to try to find Ramdas, the only person he knew in this town, and the only one who had given him any useful advice. At the building there was the same noise and bustle, but a new shift of workers had taken over and Lalu could not find Ramdas. He was so tired, and his spirits were so low, that he walked on as if in a dream without any plans or a goal of any kind. He simply let himself drift with the stream of people in the streets until suddenly, as if by a miracle, he found himself standing in front of the Taj Mahal.

Lalu did not know that the Taj Mahal was a place to which people came from all over the whole world—a place well known in every country for its beauty. It came upon him suddenly in the midst of this harsh town which had pushed him about the whole day. He felt as if he were in paradise, and stood there spellbound, rooted to the spot.

Nani had of course told him many times about the Great Mogul, who several hundred years ago had built a memorial to his dead wife. It was a mighty memorial, decorated with jewels, which had taken eighteen thousand slaves eighteen years to build. But he did not realize that it was here, and he had not dreamed that it could be as magnificent as this.

A garden, miraculously green in the hot sunshine, stretched out in front of him with flowering bushes as high as trees and tall-stemmed roses in full bloom. Long lakes of clear water, one behind the other, mirrored buildings so mighty that they took his breath away. Tall

cupolas, blinding in their whiteness, filled the sky. They must be mountains from the Himalayas, thought Lalu, which Indra had decided to plant here long ages ago. Perhaps that was why they looked so light, almost as if they were hanging in air. Forgotten was the guard who had kept him from entering the hospital, the uncle who had left the city. These large arches, fragile as lace, blotted out reality and the trials of his life and made him think only of endless beauty and peace.

He walked along the lakes looking at the temple, first as it was mirrored in the water, then as it rose against the sky, and both views were equally lovely and perfect.

People were taking off their shoes before entering the temple itself and Lalu, who had no shoes to take off, followed them. It was so dark inside that he could not see the tops of the arches. It was like standing beneath a black, starless sky. In the chamber lay buried the dead wife of the Great Mogul. One of the priests whose duty it was to look after this holy place gave a shout. Its echo bounced from wall to wall, mounting into a great noise that grew stronger the higher it rose. It was as if the sound were seeking an opening high up in the stone arches, through which it could fly out to high heaven itself.

"Perhaps," thought Lalu, "there is a path to heaven up there." And he sent a quick prayer up after the shout.

"Help us, Chaya, goddess of shade and mercy. Perhaps it was my fault that Maya did not get into the hospital. I wanted her to get well for my own sake. Help us now for Maya's sake!"

The shout rose and grew stronger and stronger as if it were trying to blast his eardrums. Lalu stood there, his head thrown back, staring after it as if he could see it. And when it died away he knew that it had taken his prayer with it.

Suddenly he understood what he must do. He must take Maya back to Asha and leave her there until he had earned enough money for the journey home. For now it was a question of her life, and her life was more important than her sight. They must go tonight, while Maya still had food in her stomach. By tomorrow she might not have enough strength left. Tomorrow, perhaps, it would be too late.

13

THE GRAY ELEPHANT

Although they did not know it, Lalu's and Maya's fate was already on its way toward them when they walked slowly away from Agra on the very same highroad by which they had come. But their fate was not in the form of a big gray elephant, as the Guru had prophesied, but rather that of a dusty gray jeep on its way to a Health Station.

The Health Station consisted of nothing but a long, unpainted wooden table set up under a mango tree. Lalu and Maya saw it ahead of them, just off the highroad, almost as soon as they began to walk that morning. They wondered why such a huge crowd of poor people—men, women, and children—were gathered around it. As they came closer, they could see that many of them were lepers with sores on their faces and on their arms. In some, the disease had gone so far that they had lost fingers and toes, and had nothing left but stumps. They were all sitting or lying as close as they could to the shadow of the tree, and were waiting patiently for something or someone to come.

Although he didn't like to get too close to lepers, Lalu was curious enough about the crowd to approach a boy on the fringe of it and ask him what they all were waiting for. The boy told him that health workers would be coming soon with injections for the lepers, and free buffalo milk for all the children. If they wanted some, all they had to do was wait. It wouldn't be long.

Lalu had no idea what health workers were, but since he and Maya were both very hungry, they decided to wait. They hadn't had anything to eat since leaving Agra the night before, and they had a long day of hard traveling ahead if they meant to reach Asha's village by nightfall.

The jeep inched its way slowly forward along the highroad through the crowded morning traffic. Behind the wheel sat an Indian lady doctor in a white sari, and at her side a Norwegian nurse and an African doctor. In the back were a huge can of ice-cold buffalo milk and two men, an American and a big, bearded Dane. The Dane, whom the others called Per, was holding the can of milk between his legs in order to make room on the seat for his body. He made the time pass quickly for his companions by telling them jokes and stories in a strange combination of English and Hindi that only made them funnier.

Per called no one by their proper name but by the name of the country which they represented. He called Astrid, the fair-haired little Norwegian nurse, *Little Norway*, the American, *Mr. U.S.A.*, and the Indian lady, who was the head of the expedition, *Beautiful Mrs. India*.

"Keep a stiff back, Little Norway, remember that you represent the World Health Organization! W.H.O.!" he shouted.

Nurse Astrid straightened herself up and laughed.

"But I represent UNICEF," said Per, holding the can of milk lovingly against himself, "and that is much grander."

This started a discussion in the jeep as to which was most important, health or food.

"Hygiene," said the American. "Cleanliness and hygiene."

"Food," said Per. "In my country nobody can think before he has had his breakfast."

"What about yourself, Per?" said Nurse Astrid. "Have you had any breakfast today?"

"Unfortunately not," said Per. "I shall have to take a sip of this buffalo milk to clear my thoughts."

Everyone under the mango tree at the Health Station, including Lalu and Maya, stood up when they saw the gray jeep coming. It emerged from a cloud of dust down the road with the blue and white banner of the United Nations flying from its roof. Then it pulled over into the

shade, moving very slowly so as not to knock down anybody in the milling crowd of people.

There was a lot of laughter over the two men who were
squeezed together with the milk can in the back seat,
until Per finally managed to worm his way out. He carried the can of milk to a table in the deepest shade, and
began the distribution, helped by Nurse Astrid.

A portable stove had been placed on the plank table,

and the water for sterilizing the syringes for the injections had now come to a boil. One by one the lepers came forward, pressed the tops of their fingers together while holding their hands in front of their faces, and saluted the lady doctor in charge of the work.

"Salaam, Memsahib, Doctor!"

Doctor Lalita Prasad, for that was her name, examined each one and entered their names in the register, helped by her two assistants who also gave the injections. Then each one was given his reward for taking the injections quietly and without complaint, namely a big mugful of buffalo milk.

But it was not so easy to get the children into line, and then make them come forward one by one in turn. Per shouted himself hoarse in his strange Hindi.

"Not a drop of milk for anyone who doesn't stand as straight as a candle. And as soon as you have gotten your milk, you must run straight home."

Finally the children obeyed him and got into line, and the distribution began. Each child was given a mugful of milk and then told to run home.

Almost at the end of the line stood Lalu and Maya with thin, one-eared Kanga between them. Nurse Astrid thought they looked more undernourished than any of the others and spoke to them in Hindi.

"What is your name?" she asked Lalu.

"Lalu," he answered in a strangely deep and adult voice.

"Lalu—that's a pretty name. And what is yours?" she asked, turning to Maya.

"Maya, daughter of Kumar Nagh of Katwa, a village east of Allahabad."

"So that is your name. Mine is Nurse Astrid."

She turned to her Danish colleague, to whom she could speak in Danish without the children understanding it.

"Look at this little girl. Isn't she pretty? But what in the world is the matter with her eyes. Do you think she's blind?"

The Dane bent down and looked into Maya's face. He held up a finger in front of her and moved it from left to right. Maya's eyes followed his hand.

"She is certainly not blind, but she soon will be," he said, shaking his head.

"Poor child!" cried Nurse Astrid. "Is it trachoma?"

"Don't know—I'm no oculist," answered Per as he gave a big mugful of milk to each of the children. He thought this a good moment for a little explanation. Best to talk about something cheerful.

"This is a present from the countries who have plenty of food to those who have not. Do you understand that?" he said to Maya.

"No," said Maya, who could not understand that it was necessary to say anything much about a mugful of milk. The only thing she understood was that it tasted good and gave her a comfortable feeling in her stomach. "But it's lovely, I know that!"

The Dane coughed.

"Far, far away from here there is a country where everyone has plenty of food. Not like here in India, where there are lots of people and very little food. If some child or other in that far-away country decides that he doesn't want an ice cream cone and gives the money to UNICEF instead—that's the name of the organization we work for—then *you* will get a glass of buffalo milk. Do you understand?"

"No," said Maya drinking her milk. "Can Kanga have a little milk, too?"

"Kanga, who's that?"

"Our dog, of course!"

"Do you hear that, Little Norway? She wants milk for her dog. If we begin to give milk to all the hungry dogs in India, we shall really have our work cut out for us!"

"Of course she shall," said Nurse Astrid who came from a country where there was plenty of food for dogs. "Look here," and she held out a saucerful to Kanga, who moved back her one ear and finished the milk in one gulp.

Per turned to Lalu.

"Do you live here?"

Lalu shook his head.

"We live in Katwa east of Allahabad and we have walked to Agra."

"You mean you have hiked?"

"No, not hiked. No one would give us a lift on the

highroad."

"So you have walked all the way from Allahabad to Agra. But why?"

"To take Maya to the hospital for her eyes. But we couldn't get into the hospital."

The two health workers exchanged glances.

"We had better speak to Dr. Prasad about this. When she's finished over there, we'll get her to take a look at these two."

Per and Astrid were soon busy distributing milk to the lepers who had had their injections. Eager hands, both with and without fingers, were streched out for the milk which was diminishing quickly.

A little later Nurse Astrid brought Dr. Prasad over. She was the most beautiful woman Lalu had ever seen. Her sari, falling in folds from her shoulders, was so dazzlingly white that it alone was a wonder in the midst of all the dust on the road. She had golden bracelets on her arms that gleamed as she moved. Her face was serious and friendly.

She turned Maya's face toward the light and looked searchingly at her eyes. Then she called the African.

"Doctor Kavuma! Come and look at this little girl!"

The African fixed a round mirror to his forehead, put his hand under Maya's chin to lift up her face, and studied her eyes. The lepers crowded around, wanting to watch. It wasn't often that a little village child was the subject of so much attention from the white-clad ones.

Then Dr. Kavuma sat on his heels in front of Maya and told her to shut her eyes. His sensitive fingers pressed her eyelids carefully, first one, and then the other. When he stood up, he spoke in English, which Maya could not understand.

"Trachoma," he said. "Early trachoma. There are already little white lumps there. Eventually both eyes will become white. Then she will be totally blind."

Nurse Astrid knelt down beside Maya and put her arm around her waist.

"Oh no, Doctor Kavuma. Not trachoma! Can't we do anything for her?"

Dr. Kavuma shrugged his shoulders. "What can we do? The eye department is full to overflowing. We haven't room for a single bed more."

"Couldn't someone be discharged to make room for this poor child?"

"Discharged in the middle of the treatment? Then *they* would become blind. It is a very long treatment. It takes time to save eyes—weeks and months."

"Couldn't her bed be put somewhere outside?" said Nurse Astrid in a troubled voice. "It's warm enough after all. The main thing is that she have treatment."

All the health workers were now standing around Maya. Lalu's eyes moved quickly from one to the other and he picked up an English word here and there that he could understand.

"Now look here, Little Norway! You can't suggest

leaving the child out of doors when the rainy season begins, and that's not far off now! You must think up something better than that!"

Nurse Astrid shook her head in a dejected sort of way. She could think of nothing else to suggest, nor did it seem any of the others could, either.

"What do you think, Beautiful Mrs. India?" asked Per.

"I think," said Dr. Prasad, "that India is the world's most unfortunate country if she can't even help her own children."

"But we can't just go off and leave these children here!"

The Dane growled into his beard: "And to think there are people in my country who believe they can't afford to help anyone but themselves!"

"It's not only in Denmark that people think like that!" said Nurse Astrid.

"We must make up our minds," said Per. "Are we going to leave them here or take them with us?"

The American settled the question.

"It seems to me that these two have performed a remarkable feat that deserves all the help we can give. There must surely be a way out!"

"America is right," shouted Sister Astrid. "There simply must be a way out!"

"But how can we even get them into the car?" asked Dr. Kavuma.

"Oh come," exclaimed Per. "They can sit on our laps.

They hardly weigh more than a letter anyhow. As for that, we might just as well send them by mail!"

Lalu sat on Dr. Kavuma's knee, Maya on Nurse Astrid's and Kanga on the floor between Per's big boots. Lalu watched eagerly as Dr. Prasad manipulated the brakes and gears and then he said:

"It wasn't a gray *elephant* that helped us but a gray *jeep!*"

14

MONKEYS IN THE APPLE
ORCHARD

When Dr. Prasad heard that Lalu had no relatives
in Agra, she took him with her to her bungalow which
lay in a lovely shady garden like so many others that
Lalu and Maya had gazed at only a few days ago. Now
he sat on the veranda, feeling utterly bewildered as he
watched Dr. Prasad pouring out tea for her guests. He
himself was given as many cakes as he could eat along
with a cup of tea sweetened with honey. When he had
finished drinking it, and had shared the last of the cakes
with Kanga, he remained sitting there gazing at his own
toes which, except for his dirty trousers, were the only
things he had left to remind him of his former life. Everything had happened so quickly that he felt very dizzy.

There was still Kanga, of course. She lay there with
her head on Lalu's lap, *his* dog from top to toe. Just a few
pounds of steadfast, stubborn faithfulness. Yes—Kanga

was real.

Otherwise everything was a dream, and almost as fantastic as the time he had gone hunting in the little weavers' forest of adventure. He felt that if he moved, even a tiny bit, he would wake up and it would all crumble around him as a dream always does. Driving to the hospital had been like a dream, too, especially when they drove past the angry guard, who meekly saluted Dr. Prasad instead of barring the way. And it had been like a dream to see Maya lying in a bed, a very small bed out in the passage among other larger beds, but still a bed, with sheets as white as the snows of the Himalayas. She had been given a bath and food, and when Lalu came up to see her, she was so sleepy that she could hardly even smile. Looking at her lying there, so peaceful and comfortable, Lalu felt as if he were free at last of the heavy burden he had been carrying for weeks. The long journey was finally over. That's why he felt so strange and giddy, as if he were floating in air, even though he was firmly planted on the floor of the memsahib doctor's veranda.

They were all there. Astrid, Per, who still went on cracking his jokes, the American, the memsahib doctor herself, and besides all these a lot of Indian doctors who talked and talked about something they called "India's Five Year Plan." Lalu vaguely remembered that he had heard about it before, over the radio that fateful day in Akvi's house, and it began to dawn on him what it all meant: hope for India's lepers . . . The World Health Organization . . . millions to be spent . . .

Everyone was very kind to him. He followed the lovely memsahib with his eyes as she went from one to the other of her guests, smiling and talking. Dr. Kavuma came in a little later and made a point of saying hello to him. Yes, they were all kind and yet Lalu felt a little forgotten as he sat there all by himself. Then the memsahib doctor smiled at him and said:

"Come and talk to me, Lalu."

Lalu got up and went over to her, followed by Kanga.

"Doctor Kavuma thinks that Maya has come soon enough so that she can be successfully treated. He thinks her eyes will get completely well, but it will take a long, long time . . . What's the matter? Do you feel ill?"

The strange dizziness in Lalu's head had increased and the whole veranda suddenly went black before his eyes. He grabbed onto the back of a chair, but would have fallen if Dr. Prasad had not caught hold of him by the arm.

"Come and sit down, Lalu. Let's sit on this step and talk a little."

Lalu tried to pull himself together. The memsahib's words, and all the talk of the others, seemed to come from very, very far away and to be part of a dream from which he must not waken. But he was so afraid he would wake up, and find them gone.

Kanga licked his face, and the memsahib doctor sat beside him quietly without speaking, giving him time to pull himself together. It was cool on the step, and the evening breeze caressed his cheeks and helped him to clear his thoughts.

"Did the news about Maya make you so happy, Lalu?"

"That's what it was," said Lalu a little shamefacedly. Then a thought struck him.

"Memsahib, will you write a letter to the Guru in our village? I can't write."

"Yes, certainly, Lalu. What shall I say?"

"Will you say that Maya is in the hospital, and will

you say that soon, after a few full moons, we shall be home."

"What more shall I write, Lalu?"

"Nothing more. When the Guru tells them about Maya, Father will know that all is well, and Nani will know that the thin branch called Lalu has not cracked on the road."

"Tell me something about your home, Lalu!"

It was strange to sit on the memsahib's veranda and talk about home. Lalu told her all about his father, who was the best farmer in Katwa; no one could stack hay as well as he could; no one else knew so much about growing rice as he did. Lalu talked about his mother, who grew vegetables in the shade of the house, and who lived in constant dread lest the little ones should get a fever and die. And he told her too about Nani, who was wiser than all the wise men put together, and about his little brothers, and about Surmi, and the buffaloes, and the roof with the stars above it, the safest place in all the world. All of this he was going back to.

Finally he told her about the journey, about all the bad things that had made them unhappy, but which no longer seemed so bad, here on the memsahib's veranda. His eyes shone with anger when he spoke of the money-lender and Akvi's ring which had caused them so much trouble and shame.

Memsahib sat and listened to it all and seemed to have plenty of time to spare.

"Soon your father will never have to go to the money-lender again, Lalu. New banks are to be opened in the villages as part of the Five Year Plan. Their interest on loans will be low, not wickedly high like the money-lender's. When they open, Akvi and her husband will be left with their money and their rings and no one will ever borrow from them again."

"That's good," said Lalu.

"Much is being done to help people in India and there are many who are helping us," said the memsahib. "It is not right that in certain parts of the world people should always have plenty to eat, while in others most of the people never have enough. But it's very difficult for people in the fortunate countries not to be selfish, Lalu."

Lalu knew this well enough. It was much easier to think only of oneself. He had realized this for a long time.

"Tell me one thing, Lalu. Did you walk all this long way just to help your sister?"

Lalu paused before he answered.

"No, not only for her sake."

"No? Why did you do it then?"

"She had been given a place in the school and I thought I could learn my letters from her."

"I see," said the memsahib doctor.

"But as we walked on and on, I began to think only of Maya's eyes. I wanted her to be like other girls, and not become like the beggars on the steps of the railway station."

"I see," said the memsahib doctor.

"Anyhow, I don't expect there are enough letters for everyone in the world to learn. I guess I shall just have to do without."

"You are a good boy," said the memsahib doctor. "There are plenty of letters in the world because we can make them ourselves, but we are short of teachers to show us how to make them."

She bent forward and patted Kanga's head.

"What are your plans now, Lalu?"

"I must get a job so as to earn enough money for our journey home."

The memsahib was still stroking Kanga.

"Since you have a dog, Lalu, I can give you a job. You can guard my apple orchard against the monkeys, who try to eat all my apples. The fruit is just getting ripe now, and the monkeys try to steal it all."

"Do you really mean I can have a job?"

"I'm sure that Kanga's bark and sharp teeth will keep the orchard free from monkeys. Of course you will have to live here if you are to guard the orchard properly. As you see, the house is overflowing with people already, but I expect we can find a little corner for you just as we did for Maya."

Very early the next morning the memsahib took Lalu to a school where the pupils sat on the floor writing on slates. A teacher stood in front of them under a huge map of India. The memsahib doctor stepped up to him, bowed, and said:

"This young man has walked all the way from Allahabad because he wants very badly to learn to read and write. I have received permission for him to come to this school, and I hope you will be able to find a place for him."

That day Lalu learned to write his own name—L-A-L-U.

When school was over, he walked home singing.

"The next letter I shall write myself, write myself," he kept repeating. "And Maya will be able to see, and her eyes will be as blue as the sea, not white like those of the beggars on the station steps."

The school was not far from the city gate, and beyond it the highroad stretched in white, shadeless sunshine as far as the eye could see. Lalu stood by the gate for a moment, gazing at the road, and felt again the old ache in the soles of his feet. The road to Agra. Snakes and starvation, tiredness and thirst. People who had been unkind and deceived him. He remembered the man with his Society for Combating Blindness, and the mere thought made him clench his fists. But he knew that the money the man had stolen could only bring him misfortune, for, as in the story Jhandu had told, he had not found it in his own hearth. And Lalu was happy when he thought of the good, honest money he was going to earn—much more than he had lost.

The road to Agra. The policemen who had chased him, and the signalman who had arrested him. But there were also the little weavers and Jhandu, Asha and

Ramdas. He would try to find Ramdas . . .

The road to Agra. So dusty and hot, blazing hot. But there had been shady places along it, too, where Kanga had danced and Maya had laughed. And then at its end the most wonderful thing of all had happened—the rescue.

"But here I'm standing, wasting time," he said, suddenly waking up to reality. "I'm forgetting my job, my fine new job!"

He turned his back on the road and, singing with joy, ran home to chase the monkeys out of the memsahib doctor's orchard.

GLOSSARY OF UNUSUAL WORDS
USED IN THIS STORY

ACACIA TREE: A tropical tree of the locust family with clusters of white or yellow flowers.

ANNA: An Indian coin worth about four cents.

AYAH: A nursemaid or governess.

BANYAN TREE: An East Indian fig tree whose branches dip down and take root in the ground.

BETEL LEAVES: Leaves from the betel palm, a tall, graceful palm tree that bears the betel nut, chewed extensively by East Indian natives.

BRAHMIN: A member of the priestly caste, the highest caste in India.

CASTE: One of the social classes into which the people of India are divided. These classes are hereditary, and very sharply defined. A member of a higher caste will usually avoid all social contact with a member of a lower one. The caste system, as it is called, is a fundamental part of the Hindu religion.

DHOTI: A long piece of material which a Hindu man winds around his legs and stomach. It is worn instead of trousers.

GANGES: Perhaps the most sacred river of India. It flows 1560 miles from the foothills of the Himalayas to the Bay of Bengal, passing the especially holy bathing site at Benares.

GHEE: Melted and strained butter obtained in India from the milk of cows or buffaloes. It is used in making and seasoning a great variety of Indian foods.

GURU: An Indian holy man or religious teacher.

JUMNA: An Indian river, 850 miles long. It flows past Agra to join the Ganges just below Allahabad.

KRAIT: A very poisonous snake of India, similar to the cobra. It is responsible for more human deaths than any other snake.

LEPER: A person suffering from leprosy, an infectious disease common among the poor and underprivileged in warm climates.

MANGO TREE: An evergreen tree of the cashew family, native to tropical Asia. It bears a yellowish-red fruit which is a vital food source to millions in the tropics.

MAHARAJAH: The title of certain Hindu princes in India.

MEMSAHIB: A lady.

NANI: A grandmother.

RUPEE: An East Indian silver coin, worth about twenty-one cents.

SAHIB: A master or lord.

SALAAM: A polite greeting in the East, performed by bowing very low and placing the palm of the right hand on the forehead.

SARI: The chief garment of a Hindu woman. It consists of a long cloth draped full in front and then wound over the bosom, the left shoulder, and sometimes also the head.

SIKH: A member of the soldier caste in India.

SIVA: One of the supreme gods of the Hindu religion.

TAMARISK TREE: A small, shrub-like tree with slender, feathery branches. Native to Southern Europe and Asia, it thrives in dry soil, and its small size makes it an excellent hedge plant.

TONGA: A light two-wheeled Indian vehicle which is drawn by a horse.

UNICEF: The United Nations Children's Fund.